STEPHANIE ROWE

Dark Wolf RISING

DARK WOLF RISING (*Heart of the Shifter #1*)
Copyright © 2015 by Stephanie Rowe
Cover design © 2015 by Kelli Ann Morgan,
www.inspirecreativeservices.com

PRINT ISBN 10: 1-940968-27-5
PRINT ISBN 13: 978-1-940968-27-8

For further information, please contact:
Stephanie@stephanierowe.com

Dedication

For Denise Fluhr, who has been there from the start.

Acknowledgements

Special thanks to my beta readers and the Rockstars. You guys are the best! There are so many to thank by name, more than I could count, but here are those who I want to called out specially for all they did to help this book come to life: Malinda Davis Diehl, Donna Bossert, Leslie Barnes, Kayla Bartley, Alencia Bates Salters, Alyssa Bird, Jean Bowden, Shell Bryce, Kelley Daley Curry, Ashley Cuesta, Denise Fluhr, Sandi Foss, Valerie Glass, Heidi Hoffman, Jeanne Stone, Rebecca Johnson, Dottie Jones, Janet Juengling-Snell, Deb Julienne, Bridget Koan, Felicia Low, Phyllis Marshall, Suzanne Mayer, Erin McRae, Jodi Moore, Ashlee Murphy, Judi Pflughoeft, Carol Pretorius, Kasey Richardson, Caryn Santee, Summer Steelman, Nicole Telhiard, Regina Thomas, and Linda Watson. Special thanks to my family, who I love with every fiber of my heart and soul.

Dark Wolf
RISING

Chapter One

BRYN McKENZIE WOULD be dead by Thursday.

And it was going to be an ugly, terrible death.

It was almost two in the morning on Christmas Eve day, and she hadn't slept yet. She just lay in bed, staring at the ceiling, waiting. Listening for the inevitable click of toenails, or a low growl, or the spine-chilling howl that would tell her that her moment had come.

Time was almost out, and she knew she would die today or tomorrow, which would be fitting, given that her own mother had died on Christmas Day. The magic of Christmas hadn't mattered to her since that horrible day, and it really wasn't foremost in her thoughts at the moment.

All she could do was lie there and frantically try to figure out a way to survive the death that was coming for her. She hadn't come up with a solution yet, despite being locked in the hotel room for three weeks. Her location was a secret...but she had no doubt that they would find her. When they did, there would be no escape.

She let out a deep breath, too exhausted and strung out to sleep, listening to the low conversation of the men in her living room.

Men who had been assigned to protect her.

Men who would fail.

They thought they knew how to keep her safe, but they hadn't seen what she had seen...which was why she had to die. No one who'd witnessed that particular murder would be allowed to live, and she knew that.

She'd known it when she'd stayed at the scene and waited for the police.

She'd known it when she'd agreed to testify at Jace Donovan's murder trial.

She'd known it when her team of highly skilled police officers had set her up in this hotel room, determined to keep her alive long enough to testify on the day after Christmas.

She'd known the risks, but she'd done it anyway. She would stay here and hope she was wrong, because a woman had died in front of her, and Bryn was the only one who knew who had done it. There was no way she could stay silent if it meant the man who'd killed that innocent woman went free. Without Bryn's testimony, the police would never have known who had murdered her. The victim's name was Melissa Stevens, a name Bryn would never forget, and the man who'd killed her was Jace Stephens...right after he shifted into a wolf.

Bryn was trying to do the right thing for once in her life. After her mom had died when Bryn was seventeen, the guilt had driven her into a self-destructive hell to hide from the pain. She'd been fighting her way back ever since, but she still felt like the shadows of the accident and the subsequent dark time in her life

2

were always haunting her. If she died trying to bring justice to the monster who'd slaughtered an innocent woman, then at least she'd die trying to do something worthy with her life.

It wasn't enough to simply *want* to make a difference. She had to *actually* make a difference. If she could stay alive long enough to testify, then maybe she could begin to understand why she'd survived the car accident that had killed her mother.

The truth was, although Bryn had accepted the risk that she might be assassinated before the trial, God help her, she didn't *want* to die, and she really didn't want to die the way Melissa had died: slowly, agonizingly, in a pool of her own blood, with her throat ripped from her body.

Bryn squeezed her eyes shut against the images that wouldn't leave her mind, the images of that horrible moment, that brutal attack, the screams that hadn't stopped ringing through her mind since it had happened. "Breathe, Bryn," she whispered, trying to slow the sudden racing of her heart. "It's okay. Right now, you're perfectly safe. No one has hunted you down yet—"

She suddenly became aware that the living room had gone silent. The men had stopped talking, and tension cut through the air, weighing on her like an iron band around her lungs.

Her heart leapt into her throat, and she bolted upright in bed. Was this it? Was it happening now? She leapt to her feet, grabbed the gun with the silver bullets from her nightstand, and backed into the corner, aiming at the door of the bedroom. She'd already dragged the heavy hotel dresser and couch in front of the door, but she knew it wouldn't save her. Her hands were shaking, and sweat was trickling down her back. She'd known they would find her, but now that they had, she couldn't control the raw fear shrieking through her mind.

There was a low growl from the living room, and she froze, fear paralyzing her. *A wolf.* Then one of the men screamed, and a frenzy of growls and snarls erupted from the living room. Gunshots. Crashes. Howls. Screams.

The men were being murdered.

She looked down at the gun in her hands, and she groaned at the sight of her shaking fingers wrapped around the metal. Highly trained professionals were being slaughtered out there, and she thought a gun would help her? She'd never even shot one before. She couldn't fight. She had to run. Now!

Frantic, she raced to the window. She was on the fifth floor. Too high to jump. She'd been happy about that at the time, knowing that no one could climb in her window, but now, dear God, now, she wished it was lower. Another crash sounded from the living room, and more gunshots.

There had to be handholds. She wasn't going to die tonight, and she wasn't going to die the way Melissa had, slaughtered by a werewolf. If she fell, at least she'd die quickly and painlessly. She shoved the gun into the waistband of her jeans and reached for the window—

A hand clamped down over her mouth and she was yanked backward, away from the window.

A silent scream caught in her throat, and she fought frantically, desperately, but whoever held her was a thousand times stronger than her. God, no, she wasn't ready to die—

"It's a rose," her captor whispered into her ear. "A white rose for friendship, a red rose for your heart, and a blue rose because the impossible is always possible."

She froze in disbelief. She hadn't heard that poem since she was fourteen, and wildly in love with her best friend, Cash Burns, who had disappeared without explanation one dark night so long ago. It couldn't be him. She hadn't heard from him or found any trace of his existence in thirteen years, and she'd tried to find him.

"It's me, Bryn," he said, his breath warm against the side of her neck. "Don't make a sound."

Tears filled her eyes as she recognized his voice, a voice she'd never thought she'd hear again. Why was Cash in her room? How was he here? She nodded once, and he immediately released his death grip on her mouth.

She spun around, and her heart seemed to stop at the sight of him. She remembered a thin, gawky fifteen year old, but standing before her, illuminated by the moonlight, was a heavily muscled man with piercing green eyes so intense they seemed to bore right through her. His dark hair was tightly cropped, no longer hanging ragged past his shoulders. His black T-shirt stretched across his muscled chest, and several long-healed scars crisscrossed his left temple. He was pure elemental male, dangerous and wildly sensual. She never would have recognized him as her childhood friend, except for his eyes, which she'd never forget. "Cash?"

Another shout echoed from the living room, jerking her attention to the door. It was closed, but the dresser and couch were ajar, showing how Cash had gotten into the room. Clearly, the heavy furniture had been nothing to him, tossed aside as easily as he used to toss her around when they'd gone swimming in the river as kids.

"It's my job to kill you. We have to make it look good." Cash pulled out a heavy knife. "Scream like I'm ripping you up." Then he dragged the knife across his forearm, spilling blood all over the carpet. "Scream. Now."

She screamed, a scream that tore from her throat and never seemed to stop. Cash was bleeding all over the carpet, taking the injury to his arm without even flinching. Good God. Who had he become? She backed away as he yanked the comforter off the bed.

"Lie down on it," he ordered. "I'll wrap you up when I take you out through there, and they won't know you're still alive. But we have to move fast. They'll be in here in seconds."

She gaped at him, a million scenarios rushing through her head. The door of the bedroom shook as something flew into it. There were fewer human screams now, and more growling and howling. "You're with them? With the werewolves? How?"

His eyes glittered. "Now, Bryn, or I can't save you." His voice was low and urgent. "They have to think you're dead."

She suddenly understood why he'd cut himself. The wolves needed to smell blood on the comforter. "Won't they know it's your blood?"

"Yeah, but they're distracted. It should be enough. For now."

She had a split second to decide whether to trust him, a man she hadn't seen in over a decade, who was now, apparently, killing people for a pack of were-wolves. He was a stranger, but he was also Cash, and he was her only chance. She'd believed in him once. She had to pray that his heart hadn't changed the way his body had. "Give me the knife."

He handed it to her without question, and she dragged it across her own forearm. He swore as she cut herself, leaping toward her and yanking the knife out of her hand. "What the hell was that for?"

"It has to be my blood. They'll know." Her knees buckled and her head spun as the pain hit. She bit her lip, fighting back gasps of pain as she cradled her arm to her chest.

He caught her, his hands framing her waist as her knees started to give out. "Shit, Bryn. You haven't changed at all." But his voice was affectionate as he helped her down to the floor. "I missed you, babe."

"You didn't miss me. You ditched me, and vanished from my life without a word." She stretched out on the floor, biting her lip when her injured arm brushed against her knee.

"I missed you," he repeated, his voice softer this time. Their eyes met, and she saw in them the person she'd once known, who she'd trusted with her life so many times before.

"You better have missed me. I'm amazing." She gripped his wrist. "If you get me killed, I'll never forgive you."

"A threat that still works with me." He winked at her, then paused just long enough to trace his fingers across her cheek. "Bryn," he said softly, his touch achingly familiar, and yet, so different from what it had once been.

A wolf howled in the living room, and he swore. "See you on the flip side, babe."

She swallowed, her mouth so dry she could barely

talk. "Okay." She kept eye contact with him as long as she could, and she didn't miss the flash of regret across his face before he flipped the blanket over her.

She sucked in her breath and rolled over, letting him truss her up in the stuffy fabric. Her arms were trapped against her sides, and her legs were locked together, entombing her in the comforter. She was utterly defenseless. Panic hit her, and she started to struggle, unable to stop herself.

"Bryn." Cash's voice was a low whisper, and she felt him touch her shoulder through the comforter. "It's just like when we were kids. Be dead."

She squeezed her eyes shut. "Just how good are you?" she asked, her voice strangled with fear. "There are wolves out there! What if they come after me?"

"I'm a serious, fucking badass, babe. I'm a thousand times what I was as a kid. I'll keep you alive, I swear." His voice radiated cocky arrogance, just like it had when they were teens, except that now his voice was deep, sliding over her skin like a sensual caress.

Heat flushed her body, and she thought back to the number of times that he'd stepped up and taken the heat for her. She remembered the way the bullies in the school always left him alone, terrified of the raw strength and power in his thin frame. Back then, he'd been the badass that no one expected, and now, he was mouthwatering muscle and man, apparently on the payroll of a pack of wolves. Which would trump, his loyalty to the pack, or to her? "What if you have to kill them to keep me alive?"

He paused for a long moment. "Then I'll kill them."

She felt the truth in his voice, and tears filled her eyes. It had been so long since anyone had stood up for her the way he always had. She hadn't realized how much she'd missed that feeling of knowing that she didn't have to fight her battles on her own. "Damn you," she said softly.

He laughed quietly, squeezing her ass through the comforter, a move that had been obnoxious when they were teens, but that now sent heat cascading through her. "I love it when I make you cry. You ready?"

She knew he wasn't asking if she was ready. He was asking if she trusted him. She let out a deep breath. Cash had always been the one she believed in, and she still did, despite the gaping emptiness of time since she'd last seen him. "Yes. Let's go."

"That's my girl." He scooped her up and slung her over his shoulder, his arm locking her down against him as he headed for the door that separated them from the wolves that had been sent to kill her.

Chapter Two

BRYN FOUGHT FOR breath in the dank, musty cocoon, her lungs aching as she heard Cash drag the dresser further away from the doorway so they could fit through it. Then she heard the door open, and the sound of the battle grew louder. She went utterly still, terrified by the thundering of her heart as he walked out into the living room. Wouldn't they hear it? The coppery scent of blood flooded her nose. She could hear the heavy panting of wolves, and the snarls and snapping of teeth, and the faint groans of humans barely alive. An overwhelming sense of grief and guilt flooded her, and she had to fight back sobs. She'd known these men, joked with them, asked them about their families, and now they were dead or dying because of her.

And this was Cash's world? How had he ever become associated with them? The urge to scream and run filled her, and she had to clench her fists to stave off the panic and will her body to stay relaxed, knowing that if she made any move, she would die instantly.

"Stand down," Cash commanded sharply, and the sounds of the wolves faded until there was only panting. She could still hear the groans of men, and she whispered a prayer that they were still alive. "Jesus, Damien." Cash's grip on her tightened, and his body was taut. "What the hell did you do here? It was supposed to be containment only. You attacked these men."

"Had to be done." Damien's voice was rough, scraping over her skin like a sharp-edged knife. "The bastards wouldn't stand down." She knew instantly that Damien was a man to stay away from, a man who was dripping with foulness and depravity. She squeezed her eyes shut, praying that he didn't realize she was still alive in the comforter.

"You done with her?" Damien asked. "The witness is dead?"

"Yeah," Cash said evenly, pitching his voice just loud enough for her to be able to hear it over the sounds of the pack growling. "I'll ditch the body where we planned."

"Change of plans." Damien sounded closer now, and she felt Cash stiffen. "I'll take her."

Cash went very still, and she felt sudden heat pour from his body through the comforter. "Who changed the plans?" he asked carefully.

"I did." Damien was so close that the darkness of his energy slid across her.

"Jace is still the pack leader," Cash said evenly, his voice like razor-sharp steel. "I take orders from him."

"Jace is in prison, so as his number two, it's my pack right now," Damien said. She felt his hand touch her back, but Cash swiftly stepped away.

"My orders," Damien said, irritation crackling

through his voice. "My call. Give me the body."

There was a long moment of silence, and Bryn's heart started hammering. Sweat was streaming down her temples. The heat Cash was generating was suffocating, her lungs straining for oxygen with each breath.

Finally, Cash spoke. "You're his number two only because I declined," Cash said, his voice so low it sounded almost like a growl. "If I decide to claim it, it's mine, so back off." Then he turned, and began to walk, his strides long and even as he walked away from Damien.

Bryn strained to listen for footsteps, but she could hear nothing more than the continued groans of men, and the panting of the wolves.

"Don't fuck with me, Cash," Damien called out.

Cash didn't turn around, and he didn't slow down. "All healers shift and stabilize the injured ones to keep them alive until the paramedics arrive," he commanded. "Everyone else clear," he ordered. "Now."

For a moment, no one responded, and then she heard Damien snap an order to the wolves. Almost instantly, she felt the energy in the room shift, and the growls turned to the low murmur of men in discussion, exchanging hurried words and orders as they hustled to do Cash's bidding. Other wolves sprang into action, their toenails clicking on the floor as they raced toward the door.

Cash turned sharply, away from the sounds, and the scent of blood and death became fainter. He moved faster, his body lithe and effortless as he sprinted down the stairs, still holding her tightly. She thought she heard the sound of canine toenails clicking on the steps, and she tried not to grunt as he ran, his shoulder digging into her belly.

He shoved open a heavy door, and then she could hear the sounds of the sirens in the distance. Should she call for help? Was that better than letting Cash take her away in a quilt? But he'd kept her alive, and the police hadn't been able to accomplish that. She *knew* him. She could trust him...except he was clearly affiliated with the wolf pack that had savaged a woman in front of her and had attacked the men assigned to protect her. What the hell was going on?

He set her down on something soft. "She's dead," he announced, loudly. "I got it covered."

"I'm coming with you." It was the voice of another man, one she didn't recognize.

Cash swore under his breath, but she heard the sounds of car doors slamming, and then the engine roared to life. Damn. Someone else was in the vehicle with them. The vehicle lurched forward, and she slid across the seat as they took off, slamming into the back of it. Her face was smashed against the back of the seat, and she could barely breathe, but she was afraid to move. Who else was with them?

Sweat was slithering down her forehead, stinging her eyes, and her arm was burning where she'd sliced it. Her lungs were aching with the need for oxygen, and she knew she was almost out of time. Her arms were pinned to her sides, and there was no way she could get out. She knew she had only a few minutes left until she suffocated. Cash needed to unwrap her, and fast.

She closed her eyes, trying to calm her frantic heart and breathe quietly enough not to give herself away. What had she done, letting a man she hadn't seen in years entomb her while her police protectors were being assassinated? The truck skidded around a corner, dumping her off the seat onto the floor, but mercifully rolling her over so her face was no longer against the seatback, allowing her to breathe ever so slightly.

"What happened back there?" The other man asked, and she squeezed her eyes shut, trying to stay calm. If the passenger was someone Cash trusted, he would have unwrapped her by now. The fact she was still trussed up on the floor could mean only one thing: the man in the vehicle with them wanted her dead.

* * *

Cash swore as he heard Bryn slide off the seat and thud on the floor as the SUV peeled around a corner. He knew he had to get her out of the comforter soon, or she'd suffocate. He was still reeling from his first sighting of her in over a decade. She still had the same blue eyes he remembered, but they weren't as innocent anymore. He hated the shadows he'd seen in them, and it had taken all his willpower to stand back and entomb her in the comforter when all he wanted to do was pull her into his arms and shield her from all the nightmares haunting her, like he used to do.

Except…his response to her was nothing like it had once been. She'd been his best friend, a girl he knew so well she was a part of him. She'd been his safe place, his source of strength, but it had never been sexual or romantic…but all that shit had gone flying out the window the moment he'd pulled her against him and felt the curves of her body, and realized that she'd become a woman. His entire body had gone hard and hot instantly, an instinctual, predatory response he hadn't been able to control.

His moment with her had been so fast, so fleeting, but it had triggered something in him that was still searing through his veins. He could still feel her body against his. Her scent was wrapped around him, filling the SUV like some siren call that made him want to vault over the seat, drag the comforter off her, and haul her into his arms and kiss her until the need pouring through him abated.

"Cash." Drake London, his best friend, disrupted his thoughts. "What the fuck went down at the hotel? I could hear the screams from the ground. I thought no one was supposed to get hurt, other than the girl." Drake was wearing black jeans, black boots, and a long-sleeved black T-shirt, dressed for the night, just like Cash. He'd been Cash's backup in case it turned out it had been a setup by Damien to take Cash out, which they'd both suspected.

The hit had turned out to be legit, but it had still been dicey as hell at the end. Cash had been a breath from calling in Drake when Damien had reached for Bryn to claim her. He'd seen the bloodlust in Damien's eyes, and he knew the other man was barely holding power over his wolf.

"I think Damien ordered them to attack," he said curtly, his mind moving at rapid speed. How the hell was he going to ditch Drake? He needed to get Bryn out of the comforter and fix her arm. He still couldn't believe she'd cut herself like that. His wolf had nearly taken control of him when she'd hurt herself. It had taken all his willpower to stay in control, when his wolf had been raging to protect her. What had she been thinking? His arm was already healing, but she was human and wouldn't heal like him. He needed to tend to her, and he couldn't do that while Drake was in the car. It was too dangerous.

"Damien ordered them to attack?" Drake frowned,

his brow furrowed in disbelief as he braced his palm on the dash and turned around to watch the road behind them. "You're sure?"

"Either that, or he let them go when they scented blood. Either way, he's responsible."

"Damien's bad news."

"No shit." Everyone knew that Damien always treaded close to the edge of bloodlust, but Jace Donovan, their alpha, always forced him to keep control. But Jace was currently locked up in prison awaiting the outcome of his trial.

Drake glanced down at Bryn's inert body on the floor. "I can't believe you killed her."

"Did my job." Cash hit the gas harder, flying down the winding road, heading deeper into the woods. He needed to put some space between himself and the rest of the pack, but he had to ditch Drake before he figured out what was up. He scanned the road, looking for a place to unload his friend.

"She was your girl," Drake observed, studying him thoughtfully. "You're too loyal to hurt anyone who matters to you."

"It was a long time ago," he muttered, still cursing that Drake had been looking right at him the moment he'd found out the name of the woman the pack was planning to assassinate. He and Drake had been together for more than a decade, a couple of fucked up kids who had scraped together a survival that neither of them deserved. Drake had been with him in those early days when he'd snuck back to Bryn's house to check on her while she was sleeping. He'd been afraid to let himself be alone with her, so he'd always brought Drake with him, with orders to do whatever it took to keep Cash from hurting her.

Of course, Cash's need to protect had been strong enough that he'd never even been close to hurting her, but his need to bring Drake as a backup had given Drake an inside look at the life he'd kept private from everyone else. When Damien had announced Bryn was the target, Drake had realized instantly that it was the same girl that Cash had guarded when they were teens.

"Maybe it was long ago, but it hasn't been long enough." Drake watched him, but Cash refused to look at him, scanning the woods up ahead. They were at least ten miles off the main road now, not far enough, but he was out of time. He had to get Bryn out of the damned quilt.

He hit the brakes, and the SUV skidded to a stop.

Drake raised one eyebrow. "What's up?"

"Get out."

His other eyebrow went up, and he didn't move. "Get out? Why?"

"Just get out."

A look of understanding dawned on Drake's face. "Son of a bitch. You didn't kill her, did you? Jesus, Cash. She's alive?" He glanced toward the backseat, his face lined with concern. "She's going to suffocate in there."

"Get the fuck out. Now." Cash reached under the seat and pulled out Bryn's gun, pointing it at his best friend. "Silver bullets, my friend."

Drake made no move toward the door. "I'm in. I'm with you. You know that."

"I won't risk you. Damien will hunt me down when they realize what I did, and he's controlling the pack right now." Cash raised the gun to eye level. "I have a gun with a silver bullet. You have no choice." His gut was eating at him for pulling a gun on the person who'd stood by him since his life had gone to hell. He knew he could use Drake's help, but he wouldn't risk his friend's life.

"They'll never believe that you would pull the trigger on me. And I don't either." Drake jerked his chin at the steering wheel. "Drive. Let's get the fuck out of here. Where are you planning to go?"

Son of a bitch. "You don't understand," Cash said. "There's nowhere safe. I won't risk your life."

Drake turned to look at him, and his eyes went cold. "I'm not going back without you, Cash. You're the only family I have. Put the fucking gun away and drive. I'll get her out." He went to lean over the seat to grab Bryn, and Cash swore and pressed the gun against Drake's temple. "No."

Drake went still, eyeing Cash. "Son of a bitch," he said softly. "You're serious."

"I won't let you die because of my choice," Cash said. "Get the fuck out."

"It's *my* choice." Drake reached into his pocket and pulled out a pocketknife. He flipped it open, moving slowly but intentionally. "While you're fucking around, she's dying back there. Shoot me if you want, but you risked everything to save her. Don't lose your shit now."

"Shit! Drake—"

His friend had already sliced open the comforter. Swearing, Cash set the gun on the dash and leaned over the back of the seat to help his friend strip the tattered remnants from Bryn. Her hair was damp with sweat, and her skin was flushed from the heat.

Fear rippled through him, and Cash yanked the last piece from her face. "Bryn!"

She sucked in a gasp, rolling onto her side. Guilt

knifed through his gut when he saw her lying there, her arm cradled to her chest, her hair tangled and damp. It took every ounce of self-control not to leap into the back and pull her into his arms. He would have if Drake hadn't been there, watching with too much insight.

She looked up at him, then her gaze flicked to Drake. There was so much fear in her eyes that he swore, fighting to suppress his wolf's need to protect her. He didn't want to scare her even more by letting her see what he was. "It's okay, Bryn. I'll shoot him if he tries to hurt you." He held out his hand, keeping his voice gentle. "Come on. Let me help."

She reached out, sliding her hand into his. Her hand was shaking, and for a split second, he was transported back to when they were kids, and he'd fished her out of a pond that she'd fallen into. Those same blue eyes, the same trust, the same trembling hand. He couldn't help but smile, and she smiled back, and for a brief second, the years vanished, and it was just them again, two lost kids counting on each other.

Then she winced in pain, and he was back in the moment, back in the middle of a high-stakes race for survival. He helped her onto the backseat, grimacing at the amount of blood still oozing from the wound in her arm. "Shit. We need to get that fixed." He sliced a section of the comforter into strips, and bound her arm to stem the flow of blood. It was crude but fast, and he was aware of Drake beside him, continuously scanning their surroundings to make sure no one was sneaking up on them.

Bryn said nothing, focused tightly on his work, her gaze occasionally flicking warily toward Drake. In less than two minutes, the wound was secure. He still needed to get it cleaned, but it would hold for now. She sank back against the seat, holding her arm to her chest, her shoulders slumped with weariness. Her tension had eased, however, and he knew that she was starting to trust him to keep her safe.

"Hey." Drake grinned at her, extending his hand over the seat. "I'm Drake London, Cash's best friend. I'm his only friend, actually. The guy's not too social."

She smiled back, faintly, warily, and shook his hand, contact that made Cash's wolf restless. Drake was his best friend, but he was also a male, and Cash's wolf didn't like him touching Bryn. "Cash has always been a loner," she said. "No one else would hang out with him except for me. You'd think he'd learn to be more popular in his old age, but I guess not."

Drake grinned. "I like you. Welcome to the party."

She smiled back. "Thanks. It seems like a great party. I'm thrilled to be here."

Drake laughed, but Cash couldn't take his eyes off her as she spoke. Her voice drifted through him, throaty and feminine, just as he remembered...except it was more. She was a woman now, not a kid. Her cream-colored tank top was tight across her breasts, and he couldn't fail to notice that she wasn't wearing a bra. Her nipples were dark circles beneath the fabric, and the swells of her breasts were easily visible. Which meant that Drake would notice as well... Possessiveness roared through Cash, and he grabbed his leather jacket from the seat beside him and handed it to her. "Here."

She raised her brows. "Thanks." She accepted it, draping it over her lap.

Her lap.

Not her breasts. Her fucking *lap*.

"So, what now?" Drake asked. "Where to?"

Cash realized he wasn't going to be able to dissuade Drake from being a part of the situation. "You're an ass," he said.

Drake shrugged. "Live with it, buddy. What's the plan?"

Cash flexed his hands on the steering wheel, thinking fast. Having Drake on his side gave them more options. "Tell Damien that you saw the body. That I ripped her up good. That I'm going to drop it on the courthouse steps on Thursday morning, when the building opens."

Drake's brows shot up. "You want me to go back to them? Damien knows we're tight. He knows I'll lie for you. If he thinks you didn't kill her, my story isn't going to change his mind."

Cash thought back to the way Damien had looked at him when he'd carried Bryn out, and he swore under his breath. "You're right. He has something going on. He'll come after me. I need to get Bryn to a safe place. Can you head him off and stall him?" He glanced in his mirror and saw Bryn's eyes widen. She looked over her shoulder, checking the dark woods.

"We need to go," she said. "They'll be coming."

"I know." He looked at Drake. "You in?"

Drake looked at them both, then swore. "Fine, but keep in touch. Tell me where to meet up. I'm not staying with the pack without you and Jace."

Cash wouldn't stay without Drake and Jace either. He nodded. "You got it."

Drake glanced back at Bryn. "Don't fuck him over, Bryn," he said softly, an edge to his voice. "He's risking everything for you."

She met his gaze. "I would never hurt him."

The steadiness of her voice made satisfaction rush through him. The bond they had was still there, maybe even stronger than it had once been. Urgency pulsed through him, the need to get her alone and away from the other male. "We need to go."

Drake saluted him and got out of the truck. His face was grim when he looked back at Cash. No words needed to be spoken aloud, but the message was clear. Drake had his back until the end, but that end might be only hours away now, despite all their years of fighting for survival. Cash had risked it all for a girl.

"I know," Cash said, acknowledging the unspoken sentiment. "Thanks. Watch your back."

"Always." Drake stepped back and slammed the door shut. Cash didn't hesitate or look back. He just hit the gas, and the vehicle exploded forward, the tires spinning as he took off, Bryn's life solely in his hands now.

Chapter Three

"HOW ARE YOU doing, Bryn?" Cash asked as he pulled out onto the road, leaving Drake standing on the edge of the woods. He hit the gas, the SUV leaping forward as they hurtled down the winding road. "Come up front."

His voice was exactly as Bryn remembered, so familiar, and yet, at the same time, so different. It was harder now. Colder. More dangerous. She still couldn't believe he'd pointed a gun at Drake. The boy she'd known would never have done that. She didn't move from her seat. "Where have you been for thirteen years?"

He met her gaze in the rearview mirror, and she saw a flash of pain in his eyes. It was gone almost immediately, replaced by an impenetrable wall that had never been there before. Then he shook his head. "How bad is your arm?" he asked, not answering her question.

"Bad, I think. The blade went deeper than I intended." What had she been thinking, slicing her arm open?

The whole scene from the hotel was surreal, like a scene from a horror flick that had left a coating of filth on her. So much blood. The screams. She'd known those men who'd been assigned to protect her. "Did they all die? Are they dead, because of me?"

He glanced back at her again, and this time, his expression was softer. "Bryn," he said gently. "The men protecting you knew the risks. It's their job. It's their lifestyle. Nothing that happened to them is because of you. They do that every day. You can't blame yourself."

"Oh, God." Tears filled her eyes as she leaned back against the seat. "They're all dead, aren't they? All of them?" Suddenly, the horror of all that had happened overtook her. She started to shake, and she felt like she was going to throw up. She couldn't stop the tears that suddenly spilled out, and she bent over, fighting back the sobs struggling to overwhelm her.

Cash swore, and she was vaguely aware of the SUV stopping. The door opened and suddenly Cash's arms were around her. "Hey, Bryn, come here."

She fell into his arms, burying her face in his neck. She was shaking so badly she felt like her body was going to shatter, but Cash pulled her tight against him, into the heated strength of his embrace. "I'm here now," he said softly, leaning his cheek against hers. "This is my world. I can keep you safe."

She squeezed her eyes shut, fighting off the sobs threatening to engulf her. His body was so strong and muscled, a solid wall of strength shielding her. She gripped the front of his shirt, holding desperately to him as she pressed her face against his chest. "I saw Jace Donovan kill that woman," she whispered. "I saw how he tore her up. It was...God. It was awful." She pulled back, searching his face for answers. "Was that what happened to those men? Was it the same?"

Cash brushed her hair back from her face, his touch so tender that new tears threatened, different tears, tears of relief at the feel of his familiar touch in the midst of so much horror. "Look at me, Bryn," he said. "What color are my eyes?"

She stared at him. "Green. Like they've always been. Why—"

"I want you to focus on me. Not on the images in your head. Think about the color of my eyes, and only the color of my eyes. Okay?"

There was no way she could do that. The images were too vivid. "I can't—"

"No." He squeezed her firmly, his hands steady on her hips. "You have to shut it out right now. We're in the open and vulnerable, and we need to stay focused."

The image of Melissa's glassy stare flashed through her mind, the expression of horror at the moment of death. She squeezed her eyes shut, but the images wouldn't stop. She was shaking now, barely able to breathe. How badly had the men suffered? How much blood had there been? "How can I not think about it? I saw it—"

He swore under his breath. "You're just as stubborn as you ever were." He slid his fingers in her hair. "Shut up and focus, babe, or I'm going to have to make you."

Her eyes flew open at the threat in his voice, and her mind leapt back to the time when she was fourteen, and he'd made that same threat. "Don't you dare, Cash—"

"Too late. I know you've been through hell, but we don't have time for you to freak out." His fingers tightened in her hair, and she knew a split second before he did it, what he was going to do.

He was going to shock the hell out of her system with a kiss designed to bring her to her knees.

* * *

Cash had meant to distract Bryn from the nightmare that wouldn't let her go.

He'd intended to use the kiss as a weapon to ground her.

He hadn't even been thinking about *enjoying* it.

But the moment he felt Bryn's lips against his, every noble thought vanished from his mind, replaced with *her*. She melted into him instantly, just as she had so long ago, kissing him back as if he was the source of the air that she breathed. The moment her body sank into his, everything inside him shifted from his mission to *her*.

Need poured through him, the kind of raw, penetrating need that obliterated everything else. The blood in his veins began to burn, and heat rushed through him, as if lava had been poured into his body and given free rein to consume him. Every thought vanished, except for his awareness of Bryn's mouth under his, and her body flush against him. Her soul seemed to envelop him as if she had become a part of him all over again. This time, however, the connection between them was on a completely different level. Before, it had been the deep bond of a friendship that would never betray him, with the first hints of sexual awakening. Now, the deep pull of their bond was just as intense, but it was inextricably intertwined with a sensuality and physical desire that almost consumed him.

"*Bryn.*" He dug his fingers into her hips and crushed her against him, deepening the kiss, ensnared by the sheer ruthlessness of his need for her. She kissed him back, just as desperately, but as deep as the kiss was, it was a brutal tease that burned for more.

He tunneled one hand through her hair, and palmed her shoulder blades with the other, as if he could, by sheer force, meld their bodies together forever. Having her in his arms again was shocking in its intensity.

In the last decade, he'd been so focused on his life, the pack, and trying to get his shit together that he hadn't had the time to focus on anything else. He hadn't had the luxury of sifting through the memories of a time in his life that, as tough as it had been, had been so much simpler, and always been bathed in the warmth of his friendship with Bryn. He'd put her, and his past, out of his mind long ago, and he hadn't thought of her again until her name had been dropped in that pack meeting that she was targeted for assassination. At that point, he'd only been thinking about making sure she didn't get killed. Not because he wanted her for himself, but because she was the one light he'd ever had, and he was going to make damn sure it didn't get extinguished.

That was it. That had been his goal. To keep her alive. Simple. Straightforward.

But now that he was kissing her, the rest of his life, his grisly, shitty life, disappeared, overwhelmed by the sheer intensity of the emotions surging through him. She wasn't a mission. She was the person who'd stood by him, the one who'd given him a reason to stay alive when the shit had hit the fan so many years ago. And now, she was in his arms, kissing him back just as fervently as he was kissing her, accepting him completely, despite the years between them, and the hell they were facing.

She made him feel human again. She made him want to be human, to care, to be more than he was, to be the guy she'd once believed in. Hopelessly ensnared by his need for her, he growled low in this throat and angled his head, deepening the kiss, needing more of her.

Bryn's arms locked around his neck, and she leaned into him, her tongue dancing with his in a frantic tango of need, lust, and desire. His cock rock hard, Cash backed her against the side of the SUV, sandwiching her between his body and the cold steel. Her breasts were crushed against his chest, her stomach tight against his. She tasted incredible, a heady combination of temptress and an innocence that was long gone from his life. Her lips were softer than he could conceive of, her kisses a siren call that sent heat rushing directly to his groin.

He moved his right hand from her shoulder blades and slid it beneath the hem of her shirt, spreading his palm across her bare skin, beneath her tank top. Electricity seemed to leap between them, a desperate siren call that had been ignited the moment he'd felt her skin against his. She sucked in her breath, her fingers tightening in his hair as he moved his hand along her lower back, tracing the lines of her spine.

He was stunned by the softness of her skin. He'd forgotten what soft was, what it felt like to do something simply because it felt good. He slid his hand over her hip, across the roundness of her ass, and back up her spine, over all the curves that made her a woman, trying to learn every bit of her body.

A low sigh escaped her lips, a sigh of desire that fueled the fire already burning with him. He moved his hand along her ribs. She shifted restlessly as he cupped

30

her breast, flicking his thumb over her taut nipple.

"Oh, God, Cash," she whispered into the kiss, tensing. "We can't do this." But she leaned into his touch, as if she needed him as much as he needed her. "They could be on us any second."

Shit. The pack. She was right. How had he forgotten? The kiss had swept everything else from his mind, literally consuming him. Swearing, he broke the kiss, but didn't let go of her. He just stared down into her face for a moment, memorizing the slope of her nose, the curve of her mouth, the thickness of her eyelashes. Regret filled him, a sadness he hadn't felt in a long time, a sense of loss for the years that he'd spent without her. "Damn," he said softly. "I think I missed you."

She laughed then, a laugh he remembered from a life that had once been his, her smile lighting up her face. He grinned, stupidly pleased that he could still make her smile, just like before. "Still a sweet-talker, I see," she teased. "You need to be, after disappearing on me like that."

His smile faded. "I'm sorry about that. I was trying to protect you."

"From what?"

He didn't answer. How could he tell her that he'd been trying to protect her from him? He didn't want her to know what he'd become.

She sighed, then touched his face, her fingers drifting gently over his cheek, as if to reassure herself he was really there. "It's good to see you, too, Cash. There's no one else quite like you."

"Is that good or bad?" He clasped her hand and pressed a kiss to her fingertips.

"Both, I expect," she replied, watching him, her face soft and vulnerable. "If I have to die tonight, I'm glad I got to see you first."

"Fuck that. You're not going to die tonight." He looked over his shoulder, reaching out with his mind to scan the night. It was quiet, empty of the energy signatures of his pack. "Let's get out of here." He began to step back, but when he saw her looking at him with her big blue eyes, something inside him shifted, a deep primal need to imprint on her, to claim her as his.

So, instead of stepping back, he hauled her against him and kissed her one more time, deep, hard, and relentless, not holding back, not hiding the fierceness that was a part of who he was. He needed her to see him for who he was, for what he was, to accept that he wasn't the kid she'd once known. He poured all he was into the kiss, not bothering to hide the raging, raw hunger that pulsed inside him, the one that her kiss had awakened.

She stiffened for a moment, and he knew she'd sensed the difference in the kiss. She knew she was in the arms of a predator, a lethal, dangerous monster. He waited, continuing his assault, his entire soul held in abeyance as he waited for her to decide how to respond.

It was a long, agonizing moment, and then she leaned into him and kissed him back, sinking her body against his once again, accepting the new side of him that he'd revealed to her. Satisfaction roared through him, and he wanted to howl with triumph. He wanted to drag her into his truck, and peel off the layers of clothing that kept them apart. He wanted to trail his mouth over every part of her body, discovering each curve and making it his. He wanted to bury himself inside her, and claim her as his own for all eternity.

His hands crept to her ass, dragging her against

him. The kiss instantly turned carnal, so intense that he felt like his skin was going to turn to fire and incinerate them both—

An owl hooted in the distance, jerking him back to the present, and to the reality that they were in a vulnerable position, out in the open, with his pack potentially on their trail. Swearing, he broke the kiss and stepped back, breathing heavily. This time, he dropped his hands from her, unwilling to trust his self-control if he was touching her. Her face was flushed, her eyes wide as she stared at him, trying to catch her breath as well.

"We need to get you safe," he said, his voice rough.

"From you?" She raised an eyebrow as she said it, and he knew she was only partially kidding. Her question was far more accurate than she had any idea.

"Babe, there's no place you can go where you'll be safe from me, now that I've found you again." He pulled the door open and indicated the front seat. "Let's do this."

For a long moment, she didn't move, searching his face, as if trying to decide how to interpret his comment. Her cheeks were still flushed from the kiss, and he could scent her arousal, which was making his cock even harder. "Bryn, if you don't get in the truck," he said quietly, "I'm going to start kissing you again, and I'm not going to stop until we're both naked. This is not the time or the place for that, but I can't help myself when it comes to you. So, get in the truck, please."

Her eyes widened. "You mean that."

"I do." For a second, he wondered what he'd do if she refused to get in the truck. It would be typical Bryn to call him on his threat to see if he was bullshitting her. He could tell she was considering it. "Not this time, Bryn. There's too much at stake. Just get in."

Her gaze slid past him, into the darkness, and then she nodded. "Okay." She ducked past him and hoisted herself into the SUV. She swiftly climbed over to the passenger side, moving with the lithe grace she'd always had. He'd always found it captivating to watch how elegantly she moved, but now, it affected him on a whole new level.

Swearing, he followed her into the truck. By the time he was seated, she was already belted in, and looking down the dark road behind them. "I don't see anything," she said.

"I don't sense them," he agreed, as he adjusted his jeans, trying to make space for his rock-hard cock. He hadn't been this turned on in a long time, and despite the degree of his discomfort, it felt good, damn good. He'd forgotten how it felt to feel like he was alive.

Bryn noticed him adjusting himself, and her eyebrows went up. She didn't make a comment, but a small smile played at the corners of her mouth as she turned away to scan the road behind them.

He was pretty sure that smile was a good sign. A really good sign. It was time to get them off the road and back to the safety of his place, and not simply to escape the pack. He wanted a few moments with her, alone, with nothing but her to think about.

But right now, he had to get them to safety. His mind refocusing on their situation, he turned on the ignition, and the engine roared to life. "Hopefully Drake can intercept the pack and give us time." Drake was highly skilled at survival and deception. The only variable was whether he could find Damien and the pack in time.

Keeping his mind attuned to their surroundings,

Cash pulled out onto the road again, shoving aside the fact that his cock and his subconscious were still fixated on the kiss and the feel of her body against his.

"Where are we going?" Bryn asked.

"I have a place where we can lay low." He noticed suddenly that she was bleeding through the comforter strips he'd bound around her arm. He nodded at her arm. "How bad is it?"

She shrugged. "It's fine. It doesn't hurt."

Her casualness made him grin. She'd always been tough, tough enough to keep up with him. Tough enough to ignore her own injuries when she shouldn't. A familiar sense of protectiveness surged through him, a need to keep her safe from her own refusal to take care of herself. "We need to stop first. You need to get treated."

She looked sharply at him. "At a hospital? Do you think that's safe?"

"No. It's not." He ground his jaw, trying to think of their best option. If Drake didn't intercept them, the pack would soon be searching for her, as would the cops. "I can take care of it. I just need to get some supplies."

"Okay. Sounds good." She smiled at him. "Thanks."

Her acceptance of his protection was automatic, reverting back to the trust they'd had so long ago. He liked that she still trusted him, despite all the time that had passed. The bond they'd had was still there...although it was different now. More powerful. More dangerous. More sensual.

She pressed her hand to her arm absently, as if she wasn't even aware she was in pain. "What's going on, Cash? Why were you there tonight? How do you know the pack? How is it that you showed up at my hotel room the night I was supposed to be murdered?"

And there it was. The questions he didn't want to answer. The truth wasn't something he wanted to share.

"Cash?"

He looked over at her, at the woman who had once been his best friend, his only friend. Her blue gaze was steady, her body relaxed as she let him escort her down the darkened road. Something shifted inside him, and he knew he wanted to tell her the truth. If anyone would believe him, it would be Bryn. If anyone would still be able to trust him after learning the truth, it would be Bryn.

But if there was anyone who could break his soul by deciding *not* to trust him upon hearing the truth…it would be Bryn.

He couldn't risk it.

Chapter Four

HE NEVER ANSWERED her questions.

It was the first time he'd ever kept secrets from her, and it made Bryn uncomfortable. What was he hiding? Why didn't he trust her with the information?

"We're stopping here." Cash pulled into the parking lot of an all-night pharmacy a short while later, parking in a spot hidden in the dark shadows by the edge of the lot. Dawn was just starting to break across the sky, a faint glow in the night that was still dark and dangerous.

Bryn scanned the empty parking lot, her discomfort with Cash's evasiveness making the night seem even more threatening. The street lights left many pockets of darkness where someone, or something, could be lurking. "You think it's safe?"

"Yeah." He shifted into park, looking around as carefully as she was. "I can sense if my pack is near. We're okay."

She glanced over at him, and she saw the truth on his face. He'd never broken a promise he'd made to her, and she believed him again. Maybe he would hide secrets from her, but he wouldn't actually lie...she hoped. What choice did she have? She'd aligned herself with him, and she had no other options than to trust him. "Okay, let's go."

He caught her arm as she started to get out, his fingers sending heat spiraling through her, despite her rising tension. "We need to stay low profile in there. A romantic couple out for a good time, that no one will associate with you or me once word gets out that a key witness for the murder trial of the century has gone missing. Got it?"

She nodded. "I promise not to talk about how I sliced my arm open to get away from a pack of murderous wolf shifters."

He flashed her a grin. "Damn, woman. I forgot about your sense of humor. No one but you can find things to joke about when the situation is this ugly."

She shrugged, knowing that her humor had been her instinctive attempt to shake the tension trying to consume her. "I'm just talented that way, I guess."

"I guess." He held out his hand to help her out of the truck. "Let's do this, sweet lips."

She raised her eyebrows at him, irritation flooding her. "Sweet lips? Really? That endearment is not nearly as innocent now that you just blew my mind with that kiss. Plus, it's kind of sexist." But she put her hand in his, and her heart fluttered when his fingers closed around hers. She'd held his hand a hundred times in her life, but this time, it felt different. His hand was so much bigger than hers, and she could feel the calluses on his palms from a rough life.

Damn him. He was sending her emotions in so many different directions, she didn't know what to think.

He winked at her, that same wink that she'd always loved. "Sorry. You bring out the worst in me."

She laughed slightly, unable to keep her tension up in the face of his familiar wink. Despite the fact that he wasn't telling her everything, he was still Cash, and he'd saved her life. She took a deep breath, and relaxed slightly. "You know damn well that I am the only person in the world who brings out your good side." She stepped out of the truck, grimacing when her bare foot landed on a pebble, reminding her that she was wearing only her leggings and camisole. The pavement was cold and hard, and her feet were freezing almost immediately. It had been unseasonably warm for December in Seattle, but not warm enough to walk around in a camisole and bare feet. "I can't go in like this. I'm not even dressed."

"I noticed." There was an edge to his voice that made her cheeks heat up, and suddenly, her camisole felt so thin and useless against the cool night air. "I'm not leaving you behind alone in the car while I go in, though." He reached into his truck, and pulled out his jacket, the one she'd had on her lap. "Wear this. We'll get you socks or something in there. They must have something."

She shrugged into his jacket, immediately enveloped in the scent of leather and man. It was warm and heavy, making her feel protected and safe. Cash wrapped his arm around her and tucked her up against his side, as they headed across the parking lot, moving quickly.

The night seemed dark and threatening, but the moment she stepped inside the pharmacy, she was hit with an overload of color, glitter, and music. A giant

Christmas tree was just inside the door, flashing brilliant colors and covered with gold garland and shiny ornaments. Christmas music blared from the ceiling, and holiday decorations were everywhere.

She stopped, shocked by the sight of it. "I forgot it was Christmas tomorrow." She'd been in that hotel for almost three weeks, trapped behind closed doors in an attempt to keep her alive. It felt so surreal to be thrust into the middle of holiday cheer. There was a display of stuffed reindeer to her right, wearing Santa hats and sunglasses. They were so ridiculous, and so familiar. Her heart softened when she saw the stuffed reindeer, and suddenly, Christmas didn't seem so far away. "You remember our first Christmas?"

Cash hadn't noticed the reindeer yet. He was looking at the signs hanging from the ceiling, no doubt scanning for the first aid section. "Yeah. You gave me the first Christmas present I'd ever had. A pair of socks. Kept those things for years. The damn things had pigs on them, and I still wore them."

She grinned at the memory of his delighted expression when he'd opened the gift. His first pair of new socks, he'd told her, and put them right on. He'd had them on almost every time she'd seen him after that, until she'd bought him another pair the next Christmas. "Do you remember what you got me?"

"Yeah. That stuffed reindeer. You told me reindeer didn't wear sunglasses. I felt like a fool, until you smiled at me, and I realized you actually liked it..." His voice faded as he saw the display in front of them. "Son of a bitch." He walked over to the display she'd seen and held one up. "It's the same one."

"Is it? It looks like it." She walked up next to him, and peered at the one in his hand. "What does the tag say its name is? Rudy?"

He flipped it over and read the tag. "Rudy," he said. "How about that? Rudy's still around." He held him up. "You still got the Rudy I gave you?"

She shook her head. "He disintegrated a few years ago."

He held it out. "Then you need a new one. Merry Christmas, Bryn."

She took the reindeer, her fingers brushing against his. It was so silly, the stuffed reindeer, but for some reason, tears filled her eyes. "Thanks."

"Hey." He brushed his finger over her cheek. "No tears, babe. Today is Christmas Eve, and you have your favorite guy back in your life."

She lifted her chin. "Yes, and we could all be torn apart in an hour. Literally."

"No different from when we were kids, right?" His eyes were dark with the memories of the life he'd had as a foster kid in so many rough situations. "You take what you can get. If you can find a good minute or two, then take it, and don't worry about what's coming, because you can't stop it anyway. Isn't that what we always said? What we always promised each other?"

She took a deep breath and nodded. "Yes, I know. It's just..." She looked at him. "It's different now, Cash. It feels like the good moments have gotten harder and harder to find."

His smile faded. "I know." He slipped his fingers behind her neck. "But we have now." He tugged her closer, and before she could react, he kissed her.

It wasn't a kiss designed to distract her, like before. It was a kiss of connection, a bond that was a part of her soul from long ago, a bond that had never left, and would always keep them connected. Being with Cash was like having her world suddenly turned right side up for the first time in a long, long time.

She slid her hand behind his neck, pulling him closer as she kissed him back. His mouth was a sinful temptation that quickly morphed from a kiss of connection to a kiss that had her wanting so much more. Desire rushed through her, a sudden fierce need that made her pull back before it could consume her.

His eyes were dark and hooded, focused on her face so intently she felt like he was seeing into her very soul. Time seemed to stand still, a frozen moment in the midst of flashing Christmas lights and blaring holiday music.

"Bryn," he whispered her name softly, his fingers tangling in her hair. His voice was so deep and sensual that it sent chills down her spine.

She swallowed. "We should go."

"I know." But he didn't move. He just studied her, as if memorizing every line of her face. It was the same way he used to look at her so long ago, as if he was certain it was the last time he'd ever see her, and he didn't want to forget. And, then, one time, it *had* been the last time they'd ever seen each other...until now.

The front door opened, and they both jumped. Cash shoved her behind him as he spun to face the door. A couple in their late teens came in, giggling and laughing, their cheeks flushed as they kissed. The boy was wearing a Santa hat, and the girl was wearing a short, red dress, as if they'd just come from a Christmas party. Harmless, teenage fun.

Bryn relaxed, but Cash didn't. He kept his body between the teens and Bryn, putting his arm around her again. "Come on, babe," he said, just loudly enough to be overheard. "I can't wait much longer to get you naked."

Her cheeks flared as he swept several boxes of condoms off the shelf as they passed the teens, who were standing near that section, giggling and looking embarrassed. "Seriously, Cash?"

"Yeah, seriously. Give them something to notice besides our faces. You've been in the news a lot. You're memorable." He guided her down another aisle to the first aid section, where he quickly loaded up, making his selections so efficiently that she knew he'd been through the drill many times before. The speed with which he selected the first aid supplies sobered her. What was his life like now? Despite the stuffed reindeer in her arms, and the desire that his kisses ignited in her, things were ugly and dangerous, and he was a part of that world. He'd been sent to kill her so she didn't testify at Jace's trial. He'd kept her alive, but how far did his loyalty go? He belonged to that pack. He'd told Damien that he could have been Jace's number two, if he hadn't declined it. Did that mean...a sudden chill rippled through her. Was he a werewolf as well? She swallowed, her heart suddenly hammering in her chest. "Cash—"

He stood up, his arms full of bandages, antiseptic, and condoms. Pink ones with extra ribbing for maximum sensation. Yellow and green stripes for the "extremely" well-endowed man. She couldn't help it. The condoms were so ridiculous that they made her laugh.

How could she doubt him? He was her best friend, her only friend, the one person on the earth she'd trust with her life. She knew he would never hurt her.

He wiggled his brows at her. "You think these are good options?"

She laughed aloud then, laughter that felt so good in the midst of such tension. "Pink? Extra sensation?"

"Hell yeah. I'm man enough for pink." He grinned at her as he nudged her toward the register. "The cashier will be more interested in the condoms and guessing what we're going to do tonight than he will be about the first aid stuff. He'll remember the condoms, not the rest of it." He snagged a pair of pale pink terrycloth slippers off a nearby rack and shot her a lecherous grin. "Besides, I never got to fulfill my raunchy teen fantasies about you. I had to take off just when I finally broke through your iron veneer. Kinda hoping to finish the job."

"You had lustful teenage boy fantasies about me?"

"Hell, yeah, of course I did." His eyes darkened. "But my imagination is a lot more dangerous now, babe," he said in a low voice.

She couldn't stop the rush of desire that cascaded through her. The teenage boy who'd been her best friend, was now pure sex and sin, and there was no way for her not to notice. "I'm celibate," she teased, trying to keep her tone light, but she couldn't quite keep the throatiness out of her voice.

"I can change that." He frowned suddenly, all amusement gone from his expression. "You're not dating anyone, are you?"

And just like that, the lightness of the mood morphed into serious, burning heat. She swallowed. "No. You?"

"Nope." He set the packages on the counter.

Nope. One casual word, and her nerve endings felt like they were on fire. She couldn't help but glance at the condoms on the counter. God, what was she thinking? Her life was in danger. This was not the time to be thinking of sex—

She noticed suddenly that the cashier had paused, inspecting the pile of medical supplies with a frown. As the man began to look up at them, Cash grabbed her wrist and hauled her against him. She threw her arms around his neck and melted into him, fire leaping through her as he kissed her.

This kiss was molten hot, burning through her body. His tongue was demanding and bold, and she met him in kind, kissing him back just as fiercely as he was kissing her. She told herself that it was okay, because it was for show, but the truth was that she wanted to kiss him desperately.

He groaned low in his chest, and locked his arm behind her back, locking her against him. Her nipples were aching with need, crushed against his chest, and she knew suddenly that the kiss wasn't for show anymore and neither were the condoms. It was a kiss that claimed her, and she realized that Cash was marking her as his, staking his claim in public, so that there could be no mistakes about who she belonged to. She'd always belonged to him, but it had been different before. Before, she'd been his best friend. This kiss staked a different kind of claim.

Adrenaline raced through her, excitement and fear twisting around each other. There was too much she didn't know about the man who had once been her best friend, too much at stake, for her to surrender to him so completely. "Cash—"

"How would you like to pay for this?" The cashier interrupted, clearing his throat.

"Cash." He released Bryn, pulled several large bills from his pocket and handed them over, his other arm still around her, holding her against him.

Her cheeks burning, Bryn stepped away from him, needing space. He received his change, grabbed the bags, and then turned toward her. His eyes were dark and brooding, shifting from the light and playful they'd been only moments before. Now, he was a predator, dark and dangerous, heading for her.

"Let's go," he said, reaching for her hand.

She hesitated, suddenly unsure. Cash was her safety net, her protector, but at the same time, he was dangerous, threatening her space and her focus.

He raised his brows. "We need to go, Bryn."

She could stay there. Have the cashier call the police. Hope that the cops could manage to keep her alive for another day...and hope that more police officers wouldn't get murdered trying to keep her alive. Or she could trust the man who ran with the wolves who'd tried to kill her, whose pack leader had already murdered a woman. Cash made her want to lose herself in his kiss and forget about everything else in the world. Could she even trust her judgment of him, or was her ability to think obscured by a friendship that had ended years ago?

The teenagers giggled behind her, and she looked back. The girl was gazing at the boy with such adoration that her heart ached. She'd once looked at Cash that way, until he'd left her. She looked at him. "I thought you were dead," she said softly. "I cried for you."

Guilt flashed across his face. "I know."

She frowned. "You know? How do you know?"

"Because I came back every night for two years to check on you while you slept. I was afraid to come back into your life, afraid of what I was, but I had to know you were okay. So, I came back."

Afraid of what he was? A wolf? An assassin? A mercenary? Something else? She'd dreamed about him sitting in her window every night, her guardian angel who'd never left. She'd thought it was dreams, but apparently, it had been real. He'd never left her. He'd always been there for her, just like he'd come back now.

She smiled, then, the last vestiges of her fear vanishing. "Okay," she said, putting her hand in his. "Where are we going?"

He wrapped his fingers around hers. "My place."

"Won't they find us?"

He shook his head as he pushed open the door. "I have a place no one knows about."

She smiled, then, remembering. "Just like the old cabin when we were kids? The one in the woods that no one knew about?"

"Same cabin. I own it now." He gave her a suggestive look that made chills pop up on her arms. "One room, Bryn. One bed." He held up the bag. "And pink is my favorite color."

Chapter Five

BRYN TUGGED THE pale pink slippers onto her feet as Cash drove them out of the parking lot. The material was soft against her cold skin, and they were the exact right size. "Did you get this size slipper on purpose?"

He glanced over at her as he pulled out onto the road. "Yeah, size eight, right? I figured the medium would fit. Why? Too small?" He frowned. "I didn't even think that your feet might have grown since then. Shit. Sorry."

"No, they fit. It's perfect." Her heart tightened. He still remembered her shoe size? It had been thirteen years. What kind of teenage boy remembered the shoe size of a girl so many years later? She sighed, trying to reconcile the man who remembered her shoe size with the lethal predator who assassinated people for a wolf pack and sliced open his arm to save a woman who'd once mattered to him. She leaned back against the seat, suddenly so exhausted, too drained to process anymore. "What's going on, Cash? Why were you there tonight? I mean, I know you were there to save me, but how do you know the pack? How is it that you showed up at my hotel room the night I was supposed to be murdered?"

Cash swore under his breath. "You don't want to know, Bryn."

She looked over at him, studying his face as he scanned the road. His jaw was hard, his face lined with tension. His long fingers were wrapped tight around the steering wheel, and she noticed scars on his knuckles. She could easily believe he was a mercenary, but whenever he spoke, she saw only the man she trusted. "I think I do," she said quietly.

He glanced over at her. "You don't."

She sighed. "Cash, I was there the day you put that boy in the hospital after he cornered me behind the school. I saw the cuts on your knuckles after you hit your foster dad when he tried to beat up that other boy in the house. I put salve on the bruises on your back from when he found you the next day. I've seen you cry when you were too scared to go back to whatever hellhole you'd been assigned to. I helped you break into your files to try to find out anything about your past or where you came from. I know that you have a dark past. I know that you're not perfect. I've always known that, but I've always loved you anyway. Why would it be different now? Just tell me. I need to know, because right now, I saw a woman get torn apart by a wolf that you appear to be trying to save. I need to understand more, Cash." She touched his arm, his biceps contracting under her fingers. "It's me, Cash. Talk to me."

He didn't look at her, but his jaw tightened. "Shit, Bryn." He sighed. "You're a pain in the ass." He sounded both irritated, and affectionate, a tone she was so familiar with from him.

"I know. That's why you love me."

"Love? Who says I love you?" He glanced over at her, and for a moment, tension hung in the air between them, a sizzling connection that hadn't been there when they were kids. Suddenly, the word "love" felt different from all the times they'd bandied it around as kids.

Then he grinned, breaking the tension. "Fine, all right, I love you, babe. You know that. Even when you make me crazy."

She smiled, settling back against the seat. Maybe love wasn't the wrong word to use for them after all. It could still mean what it had meant so long ago, that they were best friends and accepted each other's eccentricities completely, and that they'd never betray the other. As for the other kind of love, the grown-up, romantic kind...that wasn't the kind of love they shared. Was it?

He sighed, and she recognized the furrow of Cash's brow, and she knew he'd decided to tell her the truth...and that it was going to be ugly.

Anticipation laced with fear rippled through her. Did she really want to know what he was doing with a pack of wolf shifters? Did she really want to know what the boy who had once been her best friend had become? He was different now. Darker. Dangerous. Possessive. And yes, sexy beyond comprehension. She'd never responded to a man the way she had when Cash had kissed her. When his kiss had turned carnal and possessive, she knew that she should have been afraid, but she wasn't. His kiss had ignited a fierce need in her, a burning, sensual need that had stripped her of all thoughts, except those of him.

She had wanted him to make love to her right then, on the side of the road, with a pack of werewolves hunting her. It was so unlike her, and yet, at the same time, it had felt like she'd finally found where she was meant to be. Sitting beside him, still tasting his kisses on her lips, still feeling his hand on her breast, was torment. She was restless and needy, consumed by him. The instinct to reach out and touch him, even to simply brush her hand along his jaw was almost over-whelming.

She'd been without him for over a decade, and yet, within minutes of finding him again, every part of her soul had lunged for him, dragging him back into her heart with relentless fury. She'd loved him as a boy, and then she'd had to let him go. Could she really trust him again? And could she believe that the trust from so long ago was still the truth?

"What do you want to know?" he asked.

The truth. She needed it all. No matter how horrific the truth was, she needed to know who he was and what he'd become. She needed to have an answer for the burning ache inside her that he'd ignited with his kisses. "Are you one of them?" she asked. "Are you a wolf shifter? Have you...killed anyone?" The moment she asked the questions, she regretted it. If his answers were yes, what was she going to do? Run away screaming? Hug him and tell him it was okay? Because it wasn't. Killing someone was never okay. And Jace had made her terrified of werewolves. Could she really see him the same way if she knew he was a wolf, one who'd preyed upon the innocent? She needed to be able to trust him. He was her only chance at survival. Maybe it *was* better not to know. Maybe.

He answered. "Yes."

Her stomach dropped. She looked at him sharply, but he wasn't looking at her. His hands were tight around the steering wheel, his face dipping into shadows and darkness as the SUV sped along, the tires humming on the asphalt like they were being carried by a thousand bees. "Yes, to which question?"

"Both. I'm a wolf shifter, and I've killed more than one person in my life."

"Oh." She swallowed, a chill creeping down her spine. He was a *werewolf.* Visions of the horrible slaughter she'd witnessed filled her mind, of the snarling, the blood, and the screams of the woman. He'd *killed* someone. More than one person. Sweat broke out on her skin, and she wrapped her fingers around the door handle, her stomach churning as she fought to remember that this was *Cash*, her best friend, not some stranger. There had to be more information that would explain it for her. "How did you become a...werewolf?"

He shrugged. "I don't know. I don't know who my parents are. You know that." His voice was hard and cold, as it always was when he was hiding emotions he didn't want to face.

Instinctively, she looked over at him. His lips were pressed tight together. Tiny lines creased the corners of his mouth, the lines that she knew appeared only when he was exercising intense control to crush his emotions. Her heart softened, and she touched his arm. He might be a werewolf, but he was also the boy who'd stood by her, never betraying her, never letting her down. She knew what his life had been like in foster care. She'd lived through that hell with him. She was the only one he'd shown his true self to, and she knew that he was doing it again. This was *her* Cash, not some random werewolf. Whatever he'd endured, whatever he'd done, she knew that he'd done everything he could to live with the honor that had been a part of him his whole life, despite everything he'd been through.

He looked over at her, and she saw the pain in his eyes. Guilt. Self-hate. The same things she'd seen when she'd first met him. Her heart ached for him, and her fear dissolved. "I know," she said softly, running her hand down his arm. "I know you have no idea where you come from. We tried so hard to find out, but you'll never know, will you?"

He shook his head. "There's no trail," he said quietly. "I kept trying for a long time. There will never be answers."

"So, forge your own path, then, just like always." She'd met him when he was hiding from his foster parents, who used to get drunk and violent in the evenings. He'd been ten years old then, skinny and lost, concealed beneath the bleachers in the football stadium at the high school. She'd been hiding from an older boy who'd been harassing her, leering at her body in a way that she had no understanding of, except to know that it felt wrong. Cash had punched the boy on her behalf, and they'd been fast friends from then on. He'd slept in her room many times, climbing in through the window when her mom was asleep. He'd gorge himself on the food she'd snuck from the kitchen for him, using her room as a respite from the hell that was his life. Her mom hadn't approved of her friendship with a trouble-making foster kid, so they'd kept it a secret, a friendship just for them for a long time, until her mom finally began to understand the true nature of Cash's beautiful heart. Then her mom had joined his support team, offering what help she could, through food, shelter, and acceptance…though she'd never allowed him to spend the night in Bryn's bed. That had been their secret.

How many times had they shared a bed over the years? Hundreds, probably, and she'd never felt safer than when he was sleeping beside her. They'd only kissed once, not because she hadn't wanted to kiss him again, but because he'd vanished two days later, never reappearing until tonight.

She brushed her fingers through his ragged hair, reverting to the casual intimacy that had once been so natural between them. "When did you know you were a werewolf?"

"The day I left town." He angled his head slightly, leaning into her touch as he drove, as if he needed the casual connection as much as she did. "Jack, my foster dad, started wailing on one of the new kids. I got pissed and went after him. He was ready for me, and he came after me with a fireplace poker. The fight got bad, and I was losing...and I turned into a fucking wolf." His jaw tightened. "I had no idea what had just happened, but suddenly I had him by the throat, a fraction of an inch from ripping his throat out. I nearly killed him."

She stared at him, trying to imagine how shocking and surreal it must have been for Cash to turn into a wolf like that, to attack someone else. How could he even have understood what was happening to him? "That must have been terrifying."

"Scared the mother-fucking-hell out of all of us. I ran, and he let me go. Never reported me as missing because he didn't want anyone to bring me back." He still wasn't looking at her, but she could feel the tension radiating off him. "I thought I was crazy," he said softly. "Shifters weren't real, right? But it kept happening again and again. I was ready to kill myself, and then I met Drake one night. He was a shifter too, another homeless kid scared shitless. When we realized there was someone else like us, we both realized we weren't insane. So, then we got serious about figuring out what the hell was going on. We found a pack."

She could imagine the horror he'd felt. Shifters hadn't been a part of societal consciousness back then. At that time, they'd been mostly legend, the stuff of fantasy and imagination. Even now, they were on the fringe of society, with most people trying to pretend they didn't exist, and most shifters wanting to stay below the radar. No one would even have known that Melissa had been murdered by a shifter if Bryn hadn't seen the whole thing, including the shifting, and recognized the man who'd done it.

Her testimony was going to change everything. After she testified, no one was going to be able to hide behind the delusions that shifters weren't real anymore. The shifters would be exposed, and society would have to deal with it, and Jace would have to face the repercussions of what he'd done.

"The pack you're with now?" she asked. "Is that the one you and Drake hooked up with?

He looked over at her, his face softening as he nodded. "It's a good group," he said. "Jace doesn't kill for sport. It's not how we do business."

Jace Donovan was a prominent Internet mogul who had more money than most countries, and he had his eye on moving into politics, as everyone knew. Being exposed as a murderer and a shifter would destroy his career and his life, and it would bring everyone he was close to under suspicion. Fear of shifters ran high, and anyone associated with them in any way would be hunted down. "You're defending him?"

"I'm not defending what he did, but I'm defending him as a human being. It's not his style." He sped up an on-ramp onto the highway and hit the gas.

Her stomach turned. "Cash, what he did—"

"I know what he did," he said sharply. "But it doesn't make sense."

She suddenly became uncomfortably aware of the fact that it was Cash's pack whose exposure was at stake if she testified. It was his friend, Jace, who would go to prison. Cash had a personal stake in it. That was why he'd been there tonight. Because he cared about Jace. Not about her. It would affect Cash if she testified as well. Her heart suddenly sank. Was his plan to keep her from testifying? Was he really there to stop her, not rescue her? Were his kisses designed to win her loyalty so that she would decide on her own not to testify? She swallowed, choosing her next question carefully, afraid to ask too much when she was alone in a car with him, when she had no chance to escape him if he decided that things weren't going to end as he needed them to end. "Why didn't you kill me?"

He shot her a look of disbelief. "What kind of question is that? I'd never kill you."

His shock was so genuine that she let out a breath of relief. Okay, then, still the Cash she knew. He definitely wasn't going to kill her. But that left Jace and the pack's future undetermined. "Then what's going on?"

"Damien, the interim pack leader, decided that the only way to keep Jace in the clear was if there were no witnesses. He set up a strike team to silently take you out." His jaw tightened. "It was supposed to be in and out, silent and clean, with you being the only casualty.

When I found out it was you, I claimed the lead role. I don't know what shit Damien pulled while I was in there with you. Those police officers protecting you should not have been harmed."

The genuine concern in his voice caught her attention. He believed in his pack, and the wolves had violated that trust. But as long as he still believed in them, her testimony against his friends would be unwelcome. She sighed, chewing her lower lip, trying to figure out what to do.

"Don't look so worried." He looked over at her. "You're under my protection, Bryn. You always were, and you always will be."

She let out a breath of relief, knowing he was speaking the truth. His loyalty to his pack was strong, but so was his loyalty to her. "Thanks."

"No thanks necessary. I owe you."

"You did this because you owe me?" She didn't like that. It felt too good to be with him, good on a personal level, like her soul had needed him to heal it. She didn't want to be an obligation. "That's why?"

He said nothing, then he looked over at her. "No," he said softly. "I'm doing this because you are the only person in the forsaken hell of my life who matters to me. Jace saved my ass, and Drake has stood by me, but no one knows me like you do. No one gives me a safe haven, Bryn. No one, except you."

Tears filled her eyes, and all of her misgivings about him and his motivation vanished. "I missed you," she said softly.

"Missed you, too." He held out his hand, and she slipped hers into his. He closed his fingers around hers and squeezed, a solid, warm grip that made her feel safe for the first time in a long time.

Chapter Six

TWO HOURS LATER, Cash watched Bryn's face as she walked up to the old cabin that they'd hidden in so many times as kids. Her eyes were wide with wonder, her face soft with memories of a time before the world got uglier than it already had been.

She traced her hand over the doorframe, where he'd carved their initials one night. "Still there."

"Yep." He reached past her, unlocked the front door, and then disarmed the extensive security system. It might look like the same, ramshackle cabin it had once been, but he'd done a few upgrades. The walls and doors were now lined with steel. There was silver threading in the glass panes, and he'd installed a hidden floor panel that opened to two tunnels, heading in different directions. It was a lair of secrecy and survival now, the only safe place he had. Even Drake had never been there, though he knew it existed.

Bryn stepped inside, and stopped, staring at the pile of clothes folded neatly on his bed. "You have my things."

He'd forgotten about that. "Yeah. I got what I could. Didn't have much time."

She looked over her shoulder at him. "You broke into my apartment and took my clothes before coming to the hotel?"

"Yeah. It wasn't hard to find out where you lived. You need to work on that. You're too findable." He toed the door shut and reset the alarm, turning on the cameras and infrared sensors. A wall of computer monitors lit up the south wall, showing him every detail of everything moving in the vicinity. He watched closely for a moment, satisfying himself that they were alone.

Only then did he turn around to face her, and his heart seemed to freeze in his chest when he saw her sitting on his bed. Aside from Bryn, back before he even owned it, no one had ever set foot in his cabin. He needed it that way. After growing up in shitty foster homes, he needed a place where he could sleep without watching his back. He needed a space that belonged only to him, where no one could ever make a single rule that he had to obey. He needed this place to be his...but as he watched Bryn sitting on his bed, it felt right to have her there with him. It had always belonged to both of them, even when she wasn't there. Something eased inside his chest, something that had been hurting for a long time.

Her hair was tangled around her shoulders, and she looked tiny in his jacket. She was holding her arm awkwardly like it still hurt. Protectiveness surged deep inside him, a need to keep her safe. It was fierce, calling out his warrior side, but at the same time, it was soft, warm, all the things he'd long ago forgotten how to feel.

He'd forgotten what she gave to him. In his crappy childhood, she'd been the one breath of life and warmth. The one thing that had made him smile. The person who had taught him what it was like to have someone care about him. He'd changed since then. He'd become a survivor. He'd done things that had forced him to become hard...and he hadn't noticed it. Until now. Until he felt the same feelings she'd brought out in him before, so long ago.

He walked over to the bed and crouched in front of her. For a long moment, he didn't even know what to say. She looked down at him, and her eyebrows went up. "What?"

He shook his head, and brushed his fingers through a lock of her hair that had fallen forward. "I forgot," he said softly. "I forgot what it feels like to be with you."

She smiled then, her face softening. "It's been a long time, but it also feels like yesterday."

He nodded. "I'm sorry I left."

Her smile faded. "I'm sorry that you turned into a murderous werewolf."

He couldn't help the laughter that burst from him at her remark. "Yeah, well, I'm sorry about that too." He nodded at her arm. "Let's take care of your wound."

"Yes, I think it needs some attention." She immediately began to shrug off his jacket, wincing when the heavy leather slid down her arm. He helped her get it off, viscerally aware that she was wearing only a thin tank top beneath it. The curve of her breasts and the dark shadows of her nipples were easily visible, and desire surged through him.

Swearing, he shoved his lust aside, instead taking her arm to inspect it. His job wasn't to seduce her. His job was to take care of his best friend, and he needed to focus on that. The fact that he couldn't stop thinking of her as a woman was his problem, not hers. He let out his breath and examined the injury. The wound was crusted with blood, but he didn't think it was too deep. "I need to clean it."

"Okay." She made no noise of protest as he began to work on it, her only sign of pain was the way she was biting her lower lip. "What's it like?" she asked. "Being a shifter? Do you..." Her gaze slipped to his. "Do you have trouble controlling it?"

He thought of the hell he went through at first. He hated what he'd been, and he didn't want her to look at him and see who he really was. He knew she'd never sit there on the bed, locking herself in his cabin with him if she knew the truth. His life had become so dark and gritty. She was too untainted for it, and he needed her to stay the way she was. She made him feel like he could breathe again, like he could pull himself away from the darkness of his life and see sunshine, even if just for a moment.

"Cash." Her voice was soft. "Tell me."

He ground his jaw, focusing on her injury. "You won't look at me the same way," he said quietly. "You're going to see a monster." He finished cleaning the wound and began to wrap it, his fingers moving deftly after all the wounds he'd had to wrap on himself over the years. "I can't handle it if you look at me like I'm a monster," he admitted. "Anyone but you."

"Cash." She touched his cheek with her free hand, and he looked up at her. His heart skipped a beat when he saw the softness in her eyes. "I'll see you. I always have. I want to know what you've endured. You've always let me carry some of your burden. Let me do it again."

He let out his breath and said nothing as he finished her arm. He wouldn't even know where to start. The only bright spot in his life was the period of time when they'd been friends so long ago. Since then, everything had just been an endless, relentless cycle of darkness, a world she didn't belong in.

She said nothing, watching him as he packed up the supplies. He set them on the counter in his kitchenette, and then turned to face her, resting his hands on the counter behind him. He didn't want her to know, but at the same time, he did. Bryn was the only one in his life who knew him before, the one person who saw him as a human being. He and Drake were tight, but they knew each other as the monsters they currently were. Somehow, he felt that if Bryn could see what he'd become, yet still see his humanity, then maybe it was still a part of him.

"When it first happened, I had no control," he finally said. It was the truth, but superficially so. There were no words to describe the depths of what it had been like to lose control of his body, his mind, his urges. "Every time I felt threatened, I shifted. I hunted when I was in wolf form. I became an animal."

She sighed in empathy, not fear. "Did you kill people? Hunt them?"

He shrugged. "I don't know. At the beginning, I didn't always have full recollection when I returned to human form. I saw news reports that confirmed my flashes of memories, though. People who had been...attacked."

She didn't look away from him. She just sat quietly, watching him, listening.

He ran his hand through his hair. "Drake and I were attacked and almost killed when we accidentally crossed into the pack's territory the first time. Young males weren't welcome. But Jace was there, and he stopped the others from killing us." He looked over at her. "He saved me, Bryn. He taught us how to control our wolves. He taught us how to become skilled fighters, not mindless killers. If we'd been a part of the pack from the start, we never would have gone through the hell we did when we were teens, but at least Jace taught us how to bring it back under control. I still have the urges, but I direct them now to outlets that I choose."

She was staring at him. "You still kill?"

He shook his head. "I haven't killed in years. Jace doesn't allow it, and he teaches all his wolves how to control it." He couldn't believe she was still sitting there, listening to him, showing no signs of fear. A sliver of hope raced through him.

"Jace doesn't believe in killing?" She raised her eyebrows. "That doesn't make sense. I saw him—" She stopped, cutting herself off.

He tensed at her reference to that hellish night. Now that they were safe, he finally had a chance to ask her about it, and hopefully get the information he needed so desperately to clear his pack leader. "What exactly did you see?" He walked over and crouched in front of her again, searching her face. "Tell me what happened that night."

Anguish filled her eyes. "I don't want to talk about it—"

Protectiveness surged through him, fury that she'd been a part of such a horror. He'd seen it once, a werewolf in a killing frenzy, and it was horrifying. "I'm so sorry, Bryn, but I need to understand what happened that night." He lightly rested his hands on her knees and squeezed. "They can't get you. You're safe here." He didn't remind her that she was sitting in the lair of a werewolf. He could control himself. She was in no danger from him. She would *never* be in danger from him.

"What about Thursday? What about when I go to court to testify?" She looked at him. "Are you going to try to keep me from testifying against him? I saw him kill a woman, Cash. How can you let that go?"

He closed his eyes at her question, knowing she was right. If Jace was guilty, he had to pay for it. But *fuck*, he couldn't be guilty. Cash wouldn't let himself even consider the possibility. There had to be something he didn't know, something that Bryn could tell him that would make it all make sense. "Bryn, please, I need to know what happened."

"You didn't answer me. Are you going to let me testify?"

He opened his eyes. "I can't let an innocent man go to prison."

Betrayal filled her eyes. "You don't believe me?"

"I believe you're telling me the truth as you saw it, but I want to know what you don't remember seeing. Was there anyone else there?" he asked quietly. "Anyone standing in the shadows, silent, still, but present?"

"No—" She cut herself off suddenly, staring at him.

His fingers tightened on her knees. "What did you just remember?" His heart froze in his chest, hoping, desperately hoping that she was going to tell him what he wanted to hear, what he knew had to be the truth, what only she would know.

"There was someone in the shadows," she said softly. "In a doorway across the street. I barely noticed him because I was watching Jace shift. But now that you mention it, I remember seeing him there, just standing quietly. I was afraid to scream, afraid that I would be next if Jace saw me, so I just melted back into the shadows and froze. The man across the way didn't move either." She ran her hand through her hair. "I forgot about him," she said, confusion in her voice. "I completely forgot about him until now. How could that happen?"

"Some werewolves have a certain level of telepathic power." He tried to keep his voice casual, when his instincts were screaming that she'd just given him the information he'd been searching for. "Did you see his face at all?"

She ran her hands through her hair, thinking. "He was tall. Broad shoulders. Wearing some sort of trench coat."

That could have been anyone. "Anything else? Anything unusual about how he looked?"

She shivered suddenly, and looked at him. "He turned his head once, and the light from the street lights fell across his face. He had a scar on his cheek, a brutal, horrible scar."

Cash bowed his head as relief surged though him so powerfully it almost knocked him down. Silently, he pulled out his phone and scrolled to a picture of Damien, the wolf who had been leading the assassination attempt on Bryn, the one who was Jace's second in command. He held it up. "Him?"

Her face paled, and she grabbed the phone, studying the picture. "Same scar," she said. "I didn't see his eyes, but the scar is the same." She looked up. "Who is it?"

"Damien." Cash stood up, flexing his legs.

Her face paled. "He was there? But he didn't stop Jace."

"No, he didn't. Just like he didn't stop the wolves from killing the police officers protecting you." Cash strode across the room again, and braced his hands on his kitchenette counter, a thousand thoughts racing through his mind. "He was there when wolves killed both times, Bryn. Those wolves would never kill anyone, except to save their own lives. Each one had willingly given an oath not to kill. Damien was there, representing a leader who would give his own life to protect an innocent from his wolves. Despite all that, they still killed, and Damien didn't even try to stop them." He turned back. "Do you understand what that means?"

She looked down at the phone again, staring at Damien's image. "You think he made them do it somehow? With mental telepathy? But how would he control so many powerful predators?"

"I don't know, but he's doing it." Cash ran his hand through his hair. The relief he felt was almost overwhelming. "It's not Jace's fault," he said softly. "He didn't do it." He looked up. "Do you understand? He didn't do it."

Bryn set his phone down. "Jace did do it," she said quietly. "There's no way to prove that Damien made him do it. Even if I testify that Damien was present, it doesn't exonerate Jace."

Cash let out his breath in frustration. She was right. So what now? "You can't testify against Jace. You can't put him away, Bryn."

She stood up. "Neither of us has any way of knowing if Damien really made him do it. I don't know that Jace is blameless. What if he's not? What if Damien's presence means nothing, other than that he was deferring to his alpha? Jace killed a woman. I saw him do it. How can I let her death just go?"

Frustration rolled through Cash. "I know Jace is innocent. Isn't that enough for you?"

"Isn't it enough?" She stared at him as she repeated his question. "How can you ask me that? I haven't seen you in thirteen years. I have no idea where your loyalties lie, but I know that when you decide to believe in someone, it's forever. I know that, because you're willing to go against your pack to keep me safe, but that also means you'd do the same for anyone who makes your short list. Jace saved your life. Don't you owe him? Won't you owe him forever?"

"Yes, I owe him, but that wouldn't include freeing him if he's a cold-blooded murderer. He's not. I know he isn't." But as he spoke, Cash replayed Bryn's words in his mind. Doubt flickered through him. She was right that his loyalty to Jace was absolute. What if she was right? What if he wanted Jace to be innocent so badly that he was willing to delude himself so he could justify freeing him?

"Do you really know it?" She walked over to him and set her hands on his hips, forcing him to look at her.

Her eyes were as blue as they'd been so long ago, framed with long, dark lashes. She stared at him, her gaze searching his, as if she could see the truths in his soul that he couldn't see for himself. "Do you have any evidence at all that Damien can influence other wolves, especially those as strong as Jace, to do something so against their nature?"

He gritted his jaw. "No. But it makes sense. I've heard of wolves who can do it. Jace never would have attacked anyone, and he would have killed his own pack member rather than let them kill. Damien was present both times when wolves acted against their nature, and he didn't stop it. That has to be what was going on."

"In your heart, or in real life?" Her voice was soft and non-judgmental, which made it impossible for him to defend against. Her fingers tightened on his waistband. "Cash, you're such a good man. You've always been so loyal. You give your heart to so few, but when you do, it's forever. You have to see with your eyes this time, and not your heart."

He searched her face. "My heart tells me that what you saw with your eyes is not the real story. I believe in him, Bryn. I know he's blameless." He slid his hands into her hair, framing her face. "You know me, Bryn. You know me better than anyone. Do you think my heart could be wrong?"

She bit her lip, searching his face for so long that he felt a part of his heart crack. He realized then that the reason he'd hunted her down was because he'd needed *her*. He'd been doubting Jace's guilt the entire time, and he needed someone to tell him whether he was right, or just being naive. She was right that once someone gained his loyalty, it was theirs forever. Was he being blind in this situation?

She was the person he needed. Bryn was savvy, smart, and a survivor. She's seen the hell of the attack, but she also knew him in a way that no one else did, not even himself. Bryn would see the truth within him. He knew that if she told him he was wrong, he would doubt himself. Bryn was his anchor, and he needed her to believe in him.

"Bryn?" His fingers tightened in her hair. "You

were there. You saw it. You know me. What does your heart say? Am I wrong? Am I just being stupid and fucked up? You know. Tell me."

Chapter Seven

CASH'S GRIP ON her hair was too tight, too desperate, showing Bryn exactly how on edge he was. He doubted himself. He doubted his instincts. Every question she'd raised about Jace's innocence was one he'd already thought of. There was no logical reason to believe his story, but at the same time, she could feel his conviction in his heart. Every piece of his soul believed in Jace's innocence. He believed in so little in this world, so the fact he'd chosen Jace to believe in meant something.

"Bryn?"

She closed her eyes and, after weeks of fighting off the memories, she allowed her mind to return to that night. She succumbed to the horrible images that she'd worked so hard to keep at bay. She put herself back in that moment, when she'd walked out of her office at three in the morning, hating her accounting job, hating her life, hating the empty condo she had to return to. She'd felt so broken, so empty, so sad, still barely surviving in the shadows of her mother's death.

She felt Cash's finger on her cheek, brushing away a tear, and she rested her head on his chest, using him as an anchor while she opened herself up to the pain of that night, the pain she'd tried so hard to ignore. "I wanted to take a short cut to the garage," she said softly. "I knew the alley was going to be abandoned that late at night, but I didn't care. I was tired of being afraid, tired of feeling dead even though I was alive. I knew it was a safe area, and I wanted to be brave enough to walk down a stupid street."

His hands trailed through her hair, and he pressed a kiss to the top of her head. "What were you scared of?"

"My life. Me. How empty I felt. I knew I had to change something, but I didn't know what." She hooked her hands over the waistband of his jeans, letting her knuckles press against the bare skin of his stomach. "I was halfway down the alley when I felt someone's presence, like I was being hunted."

His fingers tightened in her hair, but he said nothing, letting her continue.

"I looked around, but I didn't see anyone." Her heart started to pound again, that cold, dry taste of true fear that had consumed her in that moment. "The streetlight above my head went out. One by one, all the lights in the alley blinked out." Her skin had started to crawl then, and fear had wrapped itself around her spine, terror crawling into her muscles. "I bolted for the nearest door, but it was locked. I knew I had to get out of there, but when I turned to run, I saw the silhouette of a man..."

The image appeared in her mind, and suddenly it became clearer. "No, not *a* man." God, how had she not remembered until now? It was so clear there had been two men, but the second one had completely vanished from her memory. "There were two, one behind the other, walking toward me. I ducked behind a dumpster, and waited, praying that they hadn't seen me. I didn't remember the second man until now, but he was definitely there."

"Tell me the details." Cash's voice was low. "Sounds. Smells. Temperature."

She pressed her forehead against the solid wall of his chest, trying desperately to remember. For the first time, she wanted to remember, because she wanted to be able to give Cash the information he needed to understand where his loyalties should lie. "It was hot. I was sweating. Humid."

"Wolves rise in temperature before they shift. It can affect the environment sometimes."

She breathed deeply. "It smelled like the deep woods, like fresh earth, even though we were in an alley. I remember thinking that it smelled good." And then... She squeezed her eyes shut, trying to bring the image into her mind. "I heard a woman singing. Her window was open. It was a beautiful song, almost angelic. The man coming toward me paused and looked. He stopped in the light from her window, and that's when I saw his face. I recognized him as Jace Donovan. He's in the paper so much that I knew who he was."

"She was singing?" Cash's fingers continued to work through her hair. "Did you recognize the song?"

"No, but it was beautiful. As she sang, I saw Jace's face began to change. It was his eyes first. They changed from brown to gold." She breathed deeply, opening her mind to that night. "Then his face began to change. He looked wild and feral. His face became more angular, his jaw more defined. It was so fast, the change, that I almost couldn't process it. One second he was a man, and the next moment, he was a wolf, teeth bared, sprinting for the fire escape that led to her apartment, growling. He'd barely shifted and he was already on the move." She squeezed her eyes shut, using Cash's strength to ground herself. "He leapt through the window. The glass shattered, falling all around me, and in my hair. She screamed and leapt out the window, racing down the fire escape to get away from him. He caught her just as she landed in front of me." Her fingers tightened on his jeans. "They were less than a yard from me, Cash. I could see the look on her face when he crushed her throat. It was so ruthless, so brutal, so...*God.*"

She pulled back, looking up at him. "Why, Cash? Why would someone do that?"

"He didn't do it," Cash said quietly. "There's more you're not seeing. Look away from the scene in front of you. What did you hear? What did you see? What was the other man doing?"

"I don't know!" She pushed away, her hands shaking as she relived the woman's horrific death. "He killed her and then shifted again, taking his human form again. He stood over her, staring down at her as he reclaimed his form, just staring at her like—" She stopped, suddenly, recalling the look on his face.

"Like what?"

She looked at Cash. "He looked shocked. He kept looking at the woman, and then his hands, and then back at her, like he was trying to figure out what had happened."

Cash nodded. "Memory lapse can happen during an uncontrolled shift, like when I was younger. What happened next?"

"He ran over to his pants, dug out his phone and called 9-1-1." She sat down on the bed and pulled her knees to her chest. "Then he turned sharply, as if he'd heard something. He looked right at the doorway where the other man had been, but he was gone. He looked up, like he was searching the rooftops, but before he could move, the police cars flooded into the alley. There were five of them, trapping him before he could go anywhere...except he did. He grabbed his clothes, and then went right up the side of the building and disappeared over the roofline."

Cash walked over and knelt beside the bed. "How long did the attack last?"

"Seconds. It was over so fast."

"And yet the cops were there almost instantly. They were already on their way when he called, weren't they? They had to have been."

She frowned, replaying the timing of the events in her mind. "Yes, they were there within a few seconds after he hung up."

"So someone else called before he did. Long enough for five squad cars to get there."

"It could have been anyone," she said, but even as she said it, her mind isolated a click, and a low murmur that she'd heard a split second before Jace had shifted, when only his eyes had changed. "Wait." She sat up, replaying it in her head. "I heard someone call, before Jace shifted. It was a man..." She closed her eyes, willing her mind to recall. "He was reporting a murder," she whispered. She opened her eyes to look at Cash. "A murder that hadn't happened yet."

He swore under his breath and pulled out his phone. He switched to his voice messages and hit play. "Was this his voice?"

A man's voice filled the room, echoing from Cash's phone. "We're going in tonight. Be there at seven." His voice slithered over her skin, the cold dangerous tones that she immediately recognized. It was the same one she'd heard in the hotel, when Cash had taken her out.

She sat up. "That's it. That's the voice I heard. Damien?"

He nodded, hope dancing in his eyes. "Damien reported the woman's murder *before* Jace had even shifted. What does that tell you?"

"He knew it was going to happen, and he didn't want to stop it. He wanted Jace to do it, and to get caught." She met Cash's gaze. "I think you're right, Cash."

He sank down on the bed next to her, pressing his face to his hands as he rested his elbows on his quads. "Son of a bitch," he said softly. "I thought I was making shit up." His shoulders started to shake. "He's innocent. Jace is innocent."

Bryn wrapped her arm around him and rested her head on his shoulder, just like they had so many times before. Cash was a badass, deadly, and lethal, but he still cared so deeply for those few who mattered to him. She decided that she wanted to meet Jace someday, because he had to be quite extraordinary for Cash to believe in him so strongly. "So, what do we do now?" she asked. She knew her testimony would damn Jace, and it wouldn't be enough to implicate Damien. But they had to find an answer by Thursday. It was Christmas Eve day now, and she was on the docket for the day after Christmas.

He palmed her thigh, spreading his fingers across her leg. "I'll have Drake track down the wolves from today. If one of them will testify that Damien forced the others to attack, it's proof he can do it."

"You think they're going to testify that they killed or attacked someone? Never."

He swore under his breath. "They will. To save Jace."

"At the risk of being outed as a murderous werewolf?"

He looked at her. "I would."

Her heart softened, and she ran her hand over his shoulder. "I know *you* would, Cash. But not everyone is you. And it wouldn't prove he did it this time, either. We need a confession. That's all that will work."

He swore. "We'll never get one. He's smart, Bryn. Extremely smart." He stood up and walked across the room, pacing restlessly. "I believe he knows you were still alive in that comforter. He got too close to me, and he's too fucking good at what he does." He turned to face her. "So what was his plan? Why did he let me take you out of there?"

She knew the answer as soon as he asked it, and she saw from the look on his face that he'd just realized it too. "Because you're the real leader of the pack, not him," she said. "He took Jace out, and you're next. You both have to be gone for him to be the alpha. Those wolves deferred to you at the hotel, not him. If you'd killed me, he would have ended it right then, and implicated you. But since you didn't, he let you go. He's planning something, Cash, something to take you down."

Cash walked over and sat beside her again, taking her hand in his. He began tracing his fingers along the back of her hands, just as he used to when they were teens, and he was working on a problem. She smiled to herself, suspecting that he hadn't even realized he was doing it.

"Killing you would have freed Jace," he said, his voice thoughtful as he continued to rub the back of her hand. "Since he needs Jace out of the picture, either he knew I wasn't going to kill you from the start, or he somehow had a way to still implicate Jace." He swore again, absently tracing circles on her forearm. "What am I missing?" he muttered. "What the hell is his plan?"

Chills ran down her spine from his caresses. Maybe he wasn't aware he was doing it, but she couldn't stop focusing on it. The casual touches that had been such a normal part of their lives back then felt so different now, sensual temptation instead of innocent friendship. She'd had a crush on him before, but now, her feelings were so much more. She couldn't stop thinking of his kisses, of the way it felt to have him touch her, of the stuffed Christmas reindeer sitting on the bed beside her.

Damn it. This was Cash she was fantasizing about, and they were facing a dire situation. It was not the time to think of kisses and seduction. She didn't even know why she was thinking about it... No, she realized. She did know why. It was because she'd been existing in hyper-vigilant mode for the last few months, ever since the attack, always expecting each moment to be her last. She'd been living in fear, haunted by nightmares, afraid of what was coming.

But Cash had taken away that fear. She knew she was safe with him, and because of that, she could think again. She could breathe deeply, revisit that murder with a clear mind, and she could appreciate the fact that she was still alive, and had another moment with the one person who still mattered to her. The truth was that there might not be a way to win, even with Cash on her side.

She might still die, but she wouldn't be alone, because Cash would stand by her and do everything he could to keep her alive.

She suddenly realized Cash was looking at her expectantly, his fingers still moving on her forearm. She grimaced, realizing that he must have asked her something. "Sorry, I wasn't listening. What did you say?"

He raised his brows. "What were you thinking about?"

She felt her cheeks heat up. "Nothing. Really. What's up?"

"Don't lie to me, babe." He sandwiched her hand between his palms. "Maybe it will help. What were you thinking?"

She looked at his expression, the unequivocal commitment in his eyes. Commitment to Jace, but also to her. Her heart tightened. "Cash," she said quietly. "If Damien is as smart as you say he is, there's no chance that he could have seen your face or heard your voice when you talk about me, and believed you would kill me. He knew you weren't going to kill me from the moment you offered to lead the assassination team."

His brows shot up. "I'm not the inexperienced kid I was when you knew me before, Bryn. I'm very good now, and there's no chance I gave it away."

"Really?" She smiled and ran her finger along his whiskered jaw. "Cash, no one has looked at me like you do. No one has ever loved me as you do. And I've never loved anyone like I love you. There's no chance that you can completely hide that. Drake figured it out—"

"Drake is my friend. He knows me—"

"Damien is your enemy. He has probably made it his job to know you even better."

"He didn't—"

She got up and stood in front of him, letting her hands rest by her sides. "Look at me, Cash. Look at me and tell me that you would kill me to save Jace's life. Say it like your life depended on me believing that you would."

He stared up at her, his green eyes searching hers. "Bryn, this is ludicrous."

"No, it's not." She put her hands on his shoulders, leaning down so she was eye to eye with him. "You don't need to worry about hurting my feelings, because I know I'm safe with you. But I want to see if you can say it in a way that makes me believe it, because if I don't believe you, then Damien didn't either, and that changes things. So say it. Make me believe it. Because I don't think you can."

His eyes darkened, and he grabbed her hips, jerking her toward him until her belly was against his chest. "I don't like this game, Bryn."

"It's not a game." She cupped his face, staring down at him. "Say it, Cash. Say it the way you said it to Damien. I have no doubt you're a badass like you say you are, but I know you better than you know yourself. I know your weaknesses, and I'm one of them."

His fingers tightened on her hips, and his eyes darkened. "I'll kill her," he said, his voice like steel. "I know her. I can get close to her." His eyes were like flint, and a cold chill rippled down her spine. She knew she was seeing the man he'd become, the one who'd had to do terrible things to survive.

"You'd kill a woman?" she asked, challenging him

the way she knew Damien would have. "You don't kill."

"I'll kill for Jace." His voice was cold and calm, not looking away from her eyes. "I owe him my life."

His words were cold. His voice was deadly. His eyes were unflinching. But, there was something in his eyes, an emotion buried so deeply that she knew he could never hide it. Tears burned at the back of her eyes. "Cash—"

"Son of a bitch." He bowed his head and pulled her close, burying his face in her belly as he wrapped his arms around her hips, locking her against him. "You're right. I fucking blew it."

She ran her fingers through his hair. "Cash," she said softly. "You've always had a side of you that was more compassionate and more caring than you wanted to believe. That's why we were friends. I couldn't have trusted someone who didn't have a good heart. It's still a part of you. You'll never let that go, and that's okay. We'll figure this out."

He pulled back, searching her face. His face was raw with emotion. It was entirely unguarded, and she was shocked by the vulnerability on his face. Silently, he reached for her, and she went down on her knees in front of him as he framed her face. "My sweet Bryn," he said, his voice rough and ragged. "I needed this. I needed you." He ran his fingers through her hair. "I was so fucking lost in this nightmare world I live in. I didn't even think I was human anymore. I needed you. I needed the way you look at me. The way you touch me. The way you believe in me." His hand slid around to the back of her neck, and his fingers gripped tightly, almost desperately. "I can't do this without you." He took her hand and put it on his chest, over his heart. "I can't do *this* without you. I don't know how to live, or even exist. You're my light, babe, and I can't do it without you anymore."

Tears filled her eyes. "Oh, Cash, you don't need me. You're so amazing just by being you—"

"*No.*" His fingers tightened around the nape of her neck. "You're my anchor, Bryn. You and no one else." Then, before she had time to react, he pulled her close and sank his mouth down onto hers in a desperate, intense kiss that stripped her of every last defense she had.

It was the kiss she'd been waiting for her whole life.

Chapter Eight

Bryn TASTED LIKE sanity, like home, like the foundation he'd been desperately seeking his entire life. Need poured through Cash, a desperation he hadn't allowed himself to feel in so long. *"Bryn."* He whispered her name into the kiss, tunneling his hands through her hair. The soft tresses fell across his skin, like silken strands woven by angels. He angled his head, deepening the kiss, unable to hold himself back. He felt as if a thousand lifetimes of discipline had shattered, leaving behind nothing but the raw, visceral need for the woman in his arms.

She wrapped her arms around his neck and leaned into him, meeting every kiss with equal need. He grabbed her hips and pulled her to her feet and onto his lap in one swift move.

When she slipped her legs on either side of his hips and sank down onto his lap, it sent every nerve into overdrive. He dug his fingers into her ass, pulling her more tightly against him, burying himself in the kiss. Her breasts were flush against his chest, her mouth a decadent temptation of sin, seduction, and perfection.

"God, I need you." He grabbed her hips and swung her to the side, tossing her down on his bed. He gave her no chance to settle, following her like a predator on a hunt after the prey that would keep him alive.

She held out her arms to him, her eyes warm as she welcomed him, inviting him to her body. Her face was so familiar, etched into his mind, burned into his soul. It had been so long since he'd seen her, and hunger roared through him, a feral urge to claim her and make her his. With a low growl, he lowered himself on top of her, sinking against her body as he took her mouth again. His kisses were ruthless now, his tongue enticing her into a tempestuous dance of raging fire and relentless heat.

He'd known this was coming the moment he'd locked her against his body in the hotel room. The way her ass had curved into him, the familiar scent that was unique to her, a combination of the outdoors, vanilla, and a faint flowery fragrance that reminded him of a spring meadow. His awareness of her had slammed into him, almost knocking the breath from his body when he'd grabbed her.

He'd been prepared to find the girl he'd been best friends with. He hadn't been prepared for a woman who brought him to his knees and awoke every primal male instinct in him, both wolf and man. He'd fought it. He'd dragged himself off her each time he'd kissed her, but he knew he was lost now. He just needed her too fucking badly, and in the safety of his cabin, there was nothing to stop them, nothing to hold him back.

"Cash," she whispered his name, a caress that sent shivers down his spine.

He broke the kiss, searching her face, straining to

find the words to reflect what he was feeling. "I missed the sound of my name on your lips," he said. "I didn't realize it until I found you again. I can't fucking live without you, Bryn. Don't make me."

She smiled then, that same brilliant smile that he'd dreamed of on his darkest nights. "You left me, remember?"

"You made me." Unable to stop himself, he kissed her again, invading her with his kisses, his tongue, his mouth. He slipped his hands beneath her camisole, his gut clenching when he felt her soft flesh beneath his palm. Her belly quivered as he traced her ribs, still kissing her ravenously as he slid his hand upward and cupped the soft swell of her breast.

She gasped, shifting underneath him. "How is it my fault?" Her question was swallowed by the kiss he couldn't seem to make himself stop. She just tasted so incredible. His human side craved the softness of her lips, the curves of her body. The wolf side of him could feel every beat of her heart. The scent of her arousal was intoxicating, dangerous, and powerful. He knew he was the one her body and soul craved.

They were friends. Best friends. But the need mounting between them was pure sex and raw lust, a thousand times deeper than friendly affection.

She hit his shoulder and turned her head enough to break the kiss. Anger flared in her eyes, surprising him enough to make him focus on her. "Why is it my fault? You're the one who left me alone to deal with my mom's death by myself. Where were you then? Where—"

He stopped, staring at her. "Your mom died? When?" Something inside him roared in protest, a dark, horrible darkness. Memories flashed through his mind, images of the kindnesses Bryn's mom had given him: making extra food at dinner so he wouldn't go hungry, talking to the school when they threatened to kick him out, allowing him to sleep on the couch when he was too broken to go home, and pretending not to notice when he slipped upstairs to crash in Bryn's room. She'd been Bryn's rock, and somehow, some-way, she'd extended that to Cash as well. Bryn's dad had been long gone, a piece of shit that had ditched her and her mom. That loss had given both Bryn and her mom an understanding of the shit Cash went through as a foster kid, forging a connection between a lost kid and a couple of females.

"You didn't know she died?" When he shook his head in numb shock, Bryn's eyebrows went up. "I thought you said you looked in on me every night."

"I did, for a couple years. Then Drake and I hooked up with Jace's pack and we moved to a different area." He tunneled his hand through her hair. "What happened?"

She looked past him staring at the wall behind him and he saw her face crumple. Fear rolled through him. "What the fuck happened, Bryn?" He tightened his grip on her hair and dragged his hand off her breast, resting it on her hip. "Tell me."

She draped her forearm across her face, blocking her eyes from him. "I was seventeen," she said softly.

He stretched out beside her, and gently lifted her arm off her face so he could see her. Before she could protest, he laced his fingers through hers, the way they used to do as kids when the night got too dark and scary for one of them.

She looked down at their entwined hands, and then she glanced at him. Her eyes were full of pain, so anguished that he felt a piece of his heart shatter. "I was driving on the highway," she said quietly. "It was raining. The car skidded. I—" She swallowed. "I overcorrected, Cash. It was so fast, spinning all over the place, and then, it flipped and we hit a tree, and..."

Tears burned in the back of his eyes, but he didn't take his gaze off her face. "I'm here. Tell me."

She rolled onto her side to face him, clutching their entwined hands against her heart. "When the car stopped moving, I looked over at her. Her face had been crushed. I couldn't even recognize her. So much blood. Just like that. She was gone. She was all I had left, and then, it was over." Tears streamed down her cheeks. "I was so lost, Cash. I didn't know what to do. I was a mess. I lost myself for so long after that. It wasn't until I saw you tonight that I felt like I could make it again."

Son of a bitch. Pain sliced through him. She'd been going through hell, and he hadn't been there for her. "I'm so sorry, sweetheart. I'm so fucking sorry." He pulled her into his arms, and she came willingly, burying her face against him as the sobs racked her body. He held her the way he used to, whispering all the words that had once given them comfort, stroking her hair and her back. She felt so small and vulnerable in his arms, tiny compared to him. He wanted to wrap himself around her and hide her in the shield of his body, protecting her from the pain, from life, from all the shitty things she didn't deserve.

"I missed you," she whispered. "It was so hard."

"I know." He locked his leg over her hips, dragging her more tightly against him as he kissed her forehead. He knew how close Bryn and her mother had been, and he couldn't imagine the guilt that Bryn had felt. She was the kindest person he knew, with a heart so full of love and compassion. It was her warmth that had drawn him in, but it also made her vulnerable. He'd sworn to protect her as a kid, and he'd fucking failed her when she'd needed him most. "If there was any way I could turn back the clock and be there for you, I would."

She pressed her face against his throat, her breath warm as the tears began to fade. "I wish I'd been there for you," she whispered. "It makes me so sad to think of you being so scared about what you were."

He closed his eyes, trying to imagine what it would have been like if Bryn had been a part of his life back then. "If you'd been there at that time, I would have killed myself."

She went still. "What?"

He pressed a kiss to her hair. "Every part of my soul, man and wolf, burns for you, Bryn. I haven't lost control to my wolf in years, but you push me to the edge. Having you in my arms, feeling your body against mine, tasting your lips...if I weren't so good at controlling my wolf, you'd be in danger. Back then, my wolf's need for you would have trumped. I would have killed myself rather than risk your life."

She pulled back, searching his face. Her cheeks were stained with tears, her blue eyes huge and vulnerable. "You would never hurt me, no matter what."

"Now, no. Back then?" He shrugged, brushing her hair back from her face. "I couldn't have come to you, Bryn. Seeing your tears and feeling your pain would have unleashed something in me that I wouldn't have been able to control." He tugged lightly on her hair. "Even now..." He cut himself off, knowing that now wasn't the time.

But she didn't let him off the hook. "Even now, what?" Her voice had become low and throaty, plunging right to his core.

He swore under his breath. "Don't look at me like that, sweetheart."

"Like what? Like I want you to kiss me again? Like I want you to kiss me like I'm the only thing in the entire world that matters? Like I want nothing more than to lose myself in your kiss, in the feel of your body against mine? Like I've never felt at peace anywhere except in your arms, in my whole life?"

He closed his eyes, and took a deep breath. "Bryn, there's a side of me you don't know. One you can't comprehend." He opened his eyes, and he knew that they had shifted from green to the amber gold of his wolf form. "I want to fuck you until neither of us can move. I want to own every inch of your body and soul. I want to claim you so completely that no man can get within a hundred yards of you without knowing you're mine." His fingers tightened in her hair. "That's my wolf talking, babe. The ruthless predator who knows only about survival and fighting for what is necessary to live...which means you."

Her eyes widened, and she caught her breath. Tension strung through the air, so taut that a single breath could sever it. Every muscle in his body was razor sharp, primed and ready to attack. "My life is hell," he said softly. "If I make love to you, I'm not letting you go, and you don't want to trap yourself in my life. I'm a fucking werewolf, Bryn. *Wolf.* I left you the first time for a reason. I'm not going to be able to walk away again."

She stared at him, and his heart seemed to congeal in his chest. He needed to drive her away, but he couldn't lose her. He needed her. He needed her on every fucking level of his soul. He'd never been a good guy, and he sure wasn't one now. "If you don't get up right now," he said, even as his leg tightened over her hip. "I'm claiming you. You won't ever be free of me."

He wanted her to throw him off her and escape. He wanted her to repudiate his lifestyle and save herself. But at the same time, he knew it would break him. He needed her, and he needed her to be willing to stand by him. If Bryn wasn't afraid of him, then he knew that there was something worth saving about himself. "Get up," he whispered, sliding his hand behind her neck to cup the soft flesh there. "Get up, get dressed, and get away from me."

She met his gaze, unresisting as he increased the pressure on the nape of her neck, drawing her closer to him. "Without you, I have nothing," she said steadily, not looking away from him. "I'm not afraid of your life. I want to be here, with you, wherever it takes us."

He wanted to give her another chance to change her mind. He fucking wanted to. But he couldn't. The moment she said those words, that moment she offered herself to him, he took it.

Chapter Nine

CASH'S KISS WAS searing intensity and raw need, so desperate that tears filled Bryn's eyes. She clung to him and kissed him back, her entire soul burning for the man in her arms. What had begun as something innocent and pure so long ago was now a tangled web of heartache, tragedy, loss, and connection. Cash had always been a part of who she was, and the sensation of his hands roaming her back and sliding beneath her camisole was incredible. With every kiss, a part of her seemed to settle, and the pain that had been etched in her heart for so long began to fade.

With a low growl that made her heart quicken, Cash rolled her onto her back. He lowered himself on top of her, pinning her beneath the muscled strength of his body. He was a lethal combination of sinewy strength, lightning-quick reflexes, and elemental danger on every level...but he had always been that way. He'd never been soft, except with her. He'd never been gentle, except with her. He'd always lived on the edge, a feral outsider, lurking on the fringes of the society that would never accept him.

But now she knew why. He'd always been a wolf, long before he'd ever shifted. He'd been different from the people who existed in sheltered, empty lives, unable to embrace the depths of who they truly were.

Cash slid his lips over her jaw, kissing down the side of her neck with fervent heat, sending desire cascading through her. Bryn trapped his hair in her fingers as he dragged his teeth over her collarbone and then lower, over the swell of her breasts, his mouth closing over her nipple through her camisole, in a searing swell of pleasure.

She arched her back, needing more, shifting restlessly beneath him as he palmed her other breast with his hand. "I want this," she whispered. "I want you."

"Are you so certain?" His fingers slid over her chest, along the lace of her camisole to the V between her breasts. He paused, tracing the lace as he kissed along the path his fingers had taken. He lifted his head to look at her, and her breath caught at the golden color of his irises. His pupils were dilated in the darkness, an animal adjusting to the low light. He looked wild and untamed, hovering on the edge of control. For the first time, she began to understand what he meant. As dangerous as he'd been before, he was different now, so much more...but so was she.

She framed his face with her hands, her heart aching for him. "I love you, Cash. I always have, but it's different now. You know that, don't you? You understand that's why I want this, right? I'm yours. I always have been, but you're mine, and I'll fight for you as much as you fight for me."

His eyes darkened to a deep amber, and then, with one effortless move, he tore open her camisole, ripping the soft fabric cleanly. The cool air hit her breasts, and her nipples hardened. He didn't move to kiss her. He simply gazed reverently at her body, his fingers brushing over her breasts. "So beautiful," he whispered.

She smiled at the awe in his voice. "They're just breasts," she teased.

He looked up at her, and there was no humor in his eyes. "They're yours, and that makes them beautiful." He cupped one in his palm and pressed a kiss to her nipple, not a kiss of seduction, but a kiss of tenderness and connection.

Tears filled her eyes, and her heart ached with longing. "How is it that you always make me feel so special? You've always been able to do that."

"Because I believe you are." He took her nipple into his mouth then, swirling his tongue around the taut peak, sending sparks of desire shooting through her belly. His mouth felt amazing on her skin, a decadent promise that made her belly clench with desire.

She instinctively arched into his kiss, needing more, wanting more. He continued his assault with his mouth, and slid his hand down her side, over her hip. He'd touched her hip hundreds of times in her life, but it was different now, burning with purpose and sensuality. She felt as though his touch had left behind a path of flames on her skin.

He moved up and kissed her neck, just below her ear, his hand moving in tempting circles on her hip. "I want more," he whispered. "I want skin. All of it. Mine."

Heat flushed her body. "Then take it."

He growled softly, and lightly bit her neck, making her jump. Then he sat up, still straddling her, and ripped off his shirt. His muscles were taut and defined, the body of a predator in prime physical condition. She instinctively reached for him, running her hands over his lean body. "You're the one who's beautiful."

He laughed then, grabbing her hands and pressing a kiss to each of her palms. "Men shouldn't be beautiful. Ruggedly handsome. Hot as hell. Blistering with sexuality."

She laughed aloud. "Blistering with sexuality? Really?"

"Damn right." He grabbed her wrists and pinned them over her head. "I've been wanting to get you naked ever since my first wet dream when I was thirteen. Don't screw it up by calling me beautiful." He kissed her again, hard, penetrating, ruthless. It wasn't until she was panting and squirming that he finally released her.

She dug her hands beneath the pillow, her chest heaving as he kissed his way down her body, over her breasts, along her ribs, across her stomach, to the waistband of her stretch pants. She caught her breath, and lifted her head to look at him.

He was watching her face, his chin brushing against the elastic. He hooked his fingers over the sides of her pants and grinned so devilishly that she burst out laughing. "And finally, she's mine," he whispered in a voice so sinister that chills prickled down her arms.

"You're terrifying," she said, swallowing hard as he began to tug her pants down.

"Damn right." He kissed her belly button, never taking his eyes off her face. "Don't ever forget it." He kissed lower on her belly, sliding her pants over her thighs.

Heat rushed through her when she realized he was taking her underwear with the pants. "You're not leaving me with any modesty?"

"Fuck that." He ripped her pants off in one swift move. "You can't hide from me, woman. It's far too late for that." Then he grabbed her thighs and dragged her across the bed toward him.

She shrieked in laughter, but the laugh died in her throat when he pressed a kiss between her legs, a kiss that made her gasp in shock. He was ruthless with his kisses, invading her body on every level, biting just hard enough to make her squirm, his tongue masterful, his fingers playing her body like he'd known it his whole life. She was utterly vulnerable to him, exposed to him in every way, completely at his mercy, and he knew it. She could tell in the possessive way he gripped her hips, in the fierceness of his kiss, in the tautness of his shoulders.

Desire built inside her, twisting more and more tightly, until she could barely even think. Pleasure seared though her, the kind of agonizing pleasure that needed relief, but each time she came close, he backed off, not giving her respite, stringing her along until she thought she was going to break. It was torturous per-fection, holding her at the precipice, owning her body and making her his. She twisted under the assault, her ankles locked around his shoulders, surrendering her-self to him. An orgasm swelled inside her, and he pulled back, cutting her off just before she went over the edge.

She opened her eyes as he sat on the edge of the bed and ripped off his boots. Perspiration beaded on his shoulders, his eyes glowing amber as he raked his gaze over her restless body as he stood up and yanked off his jeans and boxers, his cock springing free.

"You're amazing, Bryn." His voice was reverent and low, almost a growl as he followed her back onto the bed, showering her with kisses so intense that she couldn't even think. "I love your body," he whispered. "You're sexy as hell. Every man's dream."

Bracing himself on his elbows, he held himself above her as he kissed her again, a ravenous, claiming kiss that made her entire body clench with need. She kissed him back, her legs instinctively parting as he sank his hips between her thighs, his cock pressing against her entrance, teasing her, tempting her.

He broke the kiss and pulled back enough so she could see him. His eyes were pure gold now, with not even a fleck of green. He held her gaze, his eyes boring into hers as he shifted his hips. "Now, you're mine," he whispered, and then plunged deep inside her.

She gasped, gripping his shoulders as he filled her. Tears welled in her eyes as he went still, watching her, waiting for her to adjust. "We finally did it, didn't we?" she said, trying to keep the tears out of her voice. It felt so right with him, a lifetime that had led to this moment. She was overwhelmed, almost afraid to feel all the emotions he was stirring up inside her.

He brushed his thumb across her cheek, wiping away a tear that had trickled free. "It ain't over yet, babe." He kissed her again, and then began to move his hips, sliding out of her with tantalizing slowness, before driving deep again.

Again and again, he thrust, always kissing her, always touching, his hands roaming her body and igniting every part of her, gliding over her breasts, her hips, and across the sensitive folds of her body, until she was so tightly strung she felt as though she were going to explode.

And then, this time, just when she was hovering on that precipice again, he plunged deep, tearing away her last vestiges of self-control and unleashing a tornado inside her. She bucked and gasped beneath him as the orgasm rushed through her, clamping down on her so ruthlessly she knew she would be lost forever in his arms and in his lovemaking.

"*Bryn.*" Cash went rigid, plunging into her as the orgasm caught him, sweeping them both into a swirling whirlwind of ecstasy. She clung to him, holding on for dear life, losing herself completely in him, in their joint orgasm, and in the connection that made her complete.

* * *

Happiness was a state that Cash had never been able to comprehend. It had always felt superficial and shallow, a mirage created by naive idealists who wanted to torment people into striving for an impossible state. But as he lay in his bed with Bryn in his arms, he was filled with a sense of satisfaction and peace that had to be pretty damn close to happiness.

She was on her side, her head resting on the front of his shoulder, tucked against his side. He tightened his arm around her, pulling her more tightly against him, and then pressed a kiss to the top of her head. He loved the feel of her body against his, and he knew he would never get tired of it.

Ever.

They'd fallen asleep after making love, and it was late evening now. Christmas Eve. Thirty-six hours from when she was supposed to show up in court.

"Cash?"

He smiled at the sleepiness in her voice. "Yes, sweetheart?"

"You know I love you, right?"

His smile faded, and his throat tightened up. They'd told each other a thousand times that they loved each other when they were younger. He was so used to saying it with her that it just slipped off his tongue without thought. But the way she'd just said it was different. It was more, the kind of love that a man would never walk away from, the kind of love that deserved to be honored and cherished. The kind of love that involved long, leisurely nights of hot, sweaty bodies, not innocent hugs of friendship. The kind of love that could destroy someone.

She poked him in the chest. "Hello? Are you there?"

"Yeah." He rolled her onto her back and settled on top of her, bracing himself just enough to keep his weight from crushing her. He tangled his fingers in her hair, studying her carefully. Her hair was lighter than it had been, and longer. Her blue eyes were the same, but there was more weight in them now. Sadness. A grim awareness of the dark side of life. She was his Bryn, but there were shadows on her soul that hadn't been there before...as there were on his.

She smiled, her face contented and peaceful. "You look very handsome."

He grinned. "That's better than beautiful, but not rugged enough."

"You're a lethal, dangerous predator who looks good enough to spend the night with?"

His smile faded at her joke. "Too accurate."

She sighed and locked her hands behind his neck, resting her forearms on his shoulders. "So, what next?"

"With us?" He wanted to snatch her up, throw her into the back of his truck, and disappear with her...but he couldn't. Not with Jace's life at stake. And the truth was that Damien still wanted her dead. She was tangled up in the grittiness of his life, and he hadn't figured out a solution.

"With Jace. With Damien."

He dropped his head, burying his face in the crook of her neck. "I don't know." While she'd slept, he'd lain beside her, wracking his brain for a solution that would clear them from Damien, but nothing worked. Even killing Damien wouldn't free Jace, and the man was too smart to be trapped in a confession. "I don't fucking know what to do."

She wrapped her arms around his head, cradling him to her. "I'm not afraid," she said softly. "I'm not afraid to die, so don't worry about that."

"What?" He lifted his head, staring at her incredulously. "You don't want me to worry about the possibility of you being killed? Are you kidding?"

She blinked. "When I told the police I'd seen Jace kill Melissa, I knew that I would most likely be killed by Jace's pack. I accepted that." She touched his face. "I've found you again, Cash. If I die, I won't be alone now."

"Jesus." He rolled off her, too tense to lie still. The idea of her dying was like an electric shock to his system, a threat so severe that he could barely think. He'd just found her. He'd just claimed her. *She couldn't die.* Sweat broke out on his forehead at the idea of her being killed. "Don't talk like that." He grabbed his jeans and yanked them on, adrenaline racing through him as he fought for control. His wolf was raging, desperate to be unleashed to protect his mate. He could feel his temperature rising, his skin prickling, his muscles burning with the need to shift and defend that which was his.

"Cash?" Bryn was staring at him, her face pale. "What's wrong?"

"Nothing." He turned away, bracing his hands on the counter of his kitchenette, fighting for control. He bowed his head and closed his eyes, gritting his teeth as he tried to clear his mind. But his wolf was angry now, enraged, on the defensive. The mere mention of her death had sent it into a rage, and it wasn't backing down.

Bryn touched his back, making him jump. He spun around and grabbed her upper arms, yanking her toward him. He crushed her against him, kissing her fiercely, pouring his wolf's anger into the kiss, claiming her, showing his wolf that she was safe, that she was his, that she wasn't in danger.

Bryn made a noise of protest and pushed at his chest. "Your skin is on fire," she gasped, her eyes wide. "I feel like you're going to burn me."

"It's my wolf." It was all he could say through his clenched teeth as he kissed her again, hard, ruthlessly. "He won't let you die." He backed her against the counter, his body hard and taut, his wolf raging to be unleashed. "I can't hold it back," he gritted out. "Son of a bitch."

Bryn grabbed his shoulders. "What do you need?"

"You." His voice was a guttural growl, his wolf fighting to get out. He knew what happened when the wolf came out on its own. It was bad, so fucking bad. He'd have no control. He'd be owned by the animal. "I need to show my wolf you're safe. That you're mine. I need to fucking mark you."

Her eyes widened. "Okay."

He fisted her hair, his vision starting to shift to black and white. "I'm not going to be gentle." He had only a minute, maybe two, until he lost the battle he hadn't lost in years.

She lifted her chin, defiance blazing in her blue eyes. "I'm not a porcelain doll, Cash. You won't break me." Before he could make a decision, she grabbed his face and dragged him down to her, kissing him fiercely.

Her kiss unleashed the predator. With a furious growl, he spun her around and shoved her up against the counter. His head was spinning, his mind fragmenting, spiraling into that place where sense and logic were crushed by animal instincts. He shoved his pelvis against her ass, cupping her breast as he fumbled for the fly on his jeans, trying to get his cock free. It took seconds, precious desperate seconds, but then his jeans were unfastened.

He grabbed her hips and dragged her back toward him. She came willingly, and she was wet and hot when he sheathed himself inside her. His body went rigid, screaming for release as he drove deep, gripping her hips with a frantic need he couldn't control. She braced her hands on the counter, arching back, encouraging him, calling him to her, pushing back toward him as he drove into her.

He grabbed her hair, pulling her head back toward him as he drove into her, pummeling her more fiercely than he could control. He knew he was being too rough, but he couldn't stop himself. His wolf was in control now, needing to dominate her and claim her. His fingers sank into the soft folds between her legs, and she gasped, her body convulsing instantly as the orgasm took her. The instant she bucked against him, he lost control, and plunged deep, his seed spilling into her with such fierceness that he roared her name as he came.

It was rough. It was brutal. It sated his wolf.

Gripping her hips, he collapsed against her, resting his cheek against her back as the orgasm shuddered its last gasp and left them both. They were both slick with sweat, and he could feel her legs trembling. He wrapped his arm around her waist to support her, guilt tearing through him as he eased himself out of her. "I hurt you, didn't I?" He swore. "Fuck, Bryn, I'm so sorry. I didn't mean—"

"Don't." She turned around to face him, sweat beading on her breasts. "You didn't hurt me."

She looked so vulnerable and innocent that something inside him cracked. Her hair was streaked with sweat, and her hands were red from griping the counter so tightly. What the fuck had he been thinking, claiming her? Dragging her into his life? She deserved so much more. He spread his hands, feeling lost and shitty. "That was my wolf. That's what I am. I—" He ran his hands through his hair, trying to pull himself together. "I didn't know it would be like that. I thought I had control. I—"

"It's okay." She put her finger over his mouth, silencing him. "You didn't hurt me. I love the fact I helped you regain control of the wolf. You did, didn't you? That worked?"

"Yeah, it did, but I don't want you to become some fuck-bunny for my wolf. You deserve more than that—"

"Shut up, Cash."

He shut up, surprised into silence.

"There's no way I could ever feel like some piece of ass to you. You're not broken, but you have a dark side. I can help with that. It's okay. I've always been here for you." She shrugged, and her cheeks flushed. "It was kind of hot, actually."

He stared at her in disbelief. "Really?"

She nodded. "I admit I was a little freaked out by how hot your skin was at first, but..." She grinned. "I adapted."

Slowly, the faintest hint of a smile curved the corner of his mouth. "You're serious. That didn't...scare you? Disgust you?"

She rolled her eyes. "Oh, for heaven's sake, Cash. Seriously? Get over your drama. It was awesome." She grabbed his face and kissed him hard, with just enough sass to let him know that she meant it.

Relief poured through him, and he slid his arms around her, kissing her back. "It's your fault, you know," he said, as he kissed his way down the side of her neck. He still felt guilty as hell. He didn't know how to make it right. He had a bad feeling that this was it, his last stand with her, because he couldn't do that to her again. "You started talking that shit about how you didn't care if you died. Don't do that again, unless you want to see me turned into a four-legged demon. Got it?"

She laughed as he scooped her up. "I might say it if I want rough, hot sex, though, just to see."

He raised his brows at the serious undertone to her comment. "You liked it."

She grinned. "I did. I mean, making love in the bed was amazing, too, but there was something about being pinned against the counter that was just...sexy as hell."

His cock immediately got hard again, and he dragged her closer, exhilaration rushing through him. "Then we might need to do it again—"

A sudden, frantic beeping cut through his comment. He swore and spun away from her, lunging for his computer. He quickly called up the screens, targeting the area that had set off his alarms. "Get dressed," he said, staring at the data on the screen. "Someone's in the tunnel, heading right for us, and they're moving fast."

Chapter Ten

BRYN RACED OVER to the bed and grabbed some clothes from the stack he'd brought from her apartment while he quickly called up the cameras in the tunnel in question. It was pitch black, too dark to see anything. He switched camera angles to find a better view. He didn't want to turn on the lights and alert them, but it was too dark to see.

"What is it?" Bryn leaned over his shoulder, staring at the cameras.

"Someone's in my tunnels, coming straight toward the cabin. They're not using lights, which means they don't need them."

She tensed. "Wolf?"

"Yeah. We have great vision in the dark."

"I thought you said no one knew about this place."

"Someone does." He'd always assumed that someone would eventually find it. That was why he'd installed the security system. But having someone actually in his tunnel felt like an assault to his sanctuary. His wolf came back to life fast and hard, ready to defend his lair.

The motion sensors in the last section of the tunnel went off. The intruder was almost at his cabin. Shit. He hit the lights, flooding the tunnels with illumination. On the screen, two wolves dropped, shielding their eyes against the sudden light. He recognized them both, and swore, shutting off the light again so they could see.

Bryn's fingers dug into his arm. "That was Jace," her voice was taut with fear. "I recognize him. What's he doing here? Isn't he in prison?"

"I don't know, but he's with Drake, so that's a good sign."

There was a sudden banging on the floor, and he heard Drake's shouts to open up.

Bryn backed up, her face pale. "They're beneath us."

"Yeah. I'll let them in." He called up the trap door on his computer, and started to punch the code to let them in when Bryn's fingers closed on his wrist. He looked up to see her face ashen. "What's wrong?"

"What if you're wrong? What if he's here to kill me? Or you? Or both of us?" Her hands were shaking now, and he realized she was remembering what she'd seen Jace do. "Or what if Damien is still controlling him? You can't let him in, Cash."

He swore, and looked down at the screen. He turned on the lights in the tunnel on a low level, enough to see them. Both men were in human form now. Drake was hammering at the trap door, but Jace was leaning against the wall of the tunnel. He looked up at the camera, letting Cash see the anguish on his face. He looked like a broken man, not like the power-ful alpha who had been Cash's rock when he was lost.

Cash wrapped his arm around Bryn's shoulder and pulled her over to him. "Look at him."

To her credit, she leaned on the computer and studied the screen, but he could hear how fast her heart was beating, and his wolf sensed her fear and paced restlessly inside him, preparing to defend her. She stood up and looked at Cash. Her face was sheet white, her eyes wide with fear. "I can't look at him and see anything but the wolf that killed Melissa. I can't do this."

He took her hands, all too aware of the escalation of Drake's shouts. Drake never would have come if it hadn't been critical, and he'd never be screaming bloody murder at the camera if shit wasn't about to explode. The stakes were high and closing fast.

"Listen to me, Bryn," he said urgently, knowing that he needed to get Jace and Drake inside, but equally attuned to her safety. "If you're afraid of Jace, I'm not sure I can keep my wolf from attacking him in your defense. Both our lives are at stake here. We need to see this through. I'll keep myself between the two of you at all times. Drake's first loyalty is to me. If shit goes down, he'll be on my side."

"Can you beat Jace? Can you stop him?"

He looked into those terrified blue eyes, and he knew the answer. Jace was bigger, more seasoned, and more brutal, but he didn't have the motivation Cash did. "With your life at stake, I would win."

She searched his face, and then finally nodded. "I need my gun. Where is it? I felt you take it from my pants at the hotel. I know you kept it."

He walked over to the kitchenette and grabbed it from the silverware drawer. He'd slipped it in there when they'd first arrived. "Don't shoot me. A silver bullet can kill me even if it doesn't hit my heart."

She took it, her hands shaking violently. "Make sure I don't have to shoot at all."

"I will." He gently turned her hands to the right, angling the gun away from him and sending heat into her hands to loosen her tense muscles. "Stand by the front door, away from the trap door." He was sure about Jace's innocence, sure enough to let him in the same room as Bryn, but he wasn't a fool. He had to give himself time to react if he was wrong.

She nodded and hurried over to the door, her fingers wrapped around the gun's handle.

He walked back over to the computer to unlock the trap door, then, just before he did, he reached under the table and pulled out the silver-bladed dagger he kept there. He fingered the rubber handle, then slid the leather holster into his back pocket.

He wouldn't allow her to suffer the hell of taking a life. If he had to strike first, he would. But as he entered the code and the trap door began to slide open, he hoped like hell he wouldn't have to make the choice to kill one of the two men he trusted. The only three people in the world who mattered to him were about to be in the same room, and losing any of them would break him. *Come on, Jace.*

He grabbed two pairs of jeans and a couple T-shirts to give to the men. The trap door began to slide open, and he walked over to it, keeping himself between the men and Bryn. He didn't dare look at her. If he did, and he saw her fear, he'd attack Jace in a heartbeat. He crouched over the opening, his skin hot. His wolf pacing just beneath the surface, and he knew that there was a chance he wouldn't be able to control his wolf if Bryn were in danger.

Could he really afford to put himself in the position

where he might lose control of the beast that had once consumed him? Could he really bring Bryn into his life? Could he risk her life by exposing her to Jace? Could he risk Jace's life by putting him in the same room with his mate, who his wolf would protect at any cost?

Then the trap door opened, and he saw Drake and Jace staring up at him, two deadly shifters he was bringing into the same room as Bryn. "Cash, Damien's—" Drake cut himself off, his eyes widening when he saw Cash, instantly recognizing how close to the surface Cash's wolf was. "You're on the edge," he said, keeping his voice quiet, so as not to trigger the wolf.

"Bryn's here." Cash's voice was low and guttural, half-wolf, half-man. He dropped the clothes in, knowing that there was no chance he'd be able to hold back if the two men were naked in front of her. "She's mine. My wolf doesn't want you in the same space."

Understanding dawned on both their faces as they caught the clothes. "What the fuck, Cash?" Jace said as he yanked on the jeans. "You know you can't afford that. What did you do?"

"Too late." Cash didn't move back from the opening. "Drake first. Slowly."

Already dressed, Drake immediately grabbed the edges of the opening and hoisted himself up, swinging effortlessly into the room. His gaze flicked toward Bryn, but he immediately turned his back on her and walked to the other side of the room, giving Cash's wolf the message that he wasn't going to challenge for her.

Jace, however, wisely stayed in the tunnel. Both men had seen Cash's wolf unleashed without control, and they both knew how dangerous he was. Cash could sense their urgency, but they stayed calm, careful not to make any move that could trigger him.

Cash looked down at Jace. "What happened?" He didn't invite Jace up. Not yet. He needed to hear it from him first.

Jace spread his hands in a helpless gesture, knowing exactly what Cash was asking. "I don't know. I couldn't stop myself. The song awakened something in me, and I lost my shit."

"The song?" Cash frowned. "It was the *song*?"

"I don't know. The minute I heard the first note, my mind became..." He grimaced. "A white rage is the best I can describe it." He looked up at Cash, his eyes an empty wasteland. "I don't know what the fuck happened, Cash. When my mind came back to me, and I saw what I'd done... Jesus, Cash. It was horrific, and I did it. *I did it.* I don't even think I should be out of that prison cell." He met his gaze. "Kill me if it starts again. Just end it."

All doubt about his faith in his alpha vanished under the weight of Jace's torment. Jace had done it, but the intent hadn't been there, and that was enough for him. Except... "Bryn's here." He watched Jace carefully for any sign that her presence would trigger him, but Jace simply nodded.

They stared at each other for a long moment, then Cash looked back at Bryn. Her face was ashen, and she was pointing the gun at them. Protectiveness surged through him, and his wolf rose again. If he had any choice, *any fucking choice*, he wouldn't let Jace up. He wouldn't take that risk. But he owed the other man his life. "Jace can't promise he won't snap again," he said to her.

Bryn squeezed her eyes shut. "Dear God, Cash. I can't do this."

"He was manipulated. He's innocent of intent. He's an innocent man, Bryn. We have to save him."

She opened her eyes. "He's also guilty."

"Never mind." Jace spoke. "I'll just go—"

"No!" Drake walked over. "It won't end if Jace leaves. He may snap again, and Damien will kill others. We have to end this today." He looked at Cash. "Damien's on his way here. He arranged for Jace's escape. He wants to catch the three of us together, kill Bryn, and then make us all hang for Bryn's death. He's on his way, Cash. He'll be here in fifteen minutes with those most loyal to him."

Jace nodded. "Drake got me free from them, and we beat them here, but we're not ahead of them by much. Damien's planning to end it now, for all four of us."

Son of a bitch. How did everyone know where his cabin was? Not that he had time to deal with that now. His place had been compromised, leaving him with no choice. They would have to work together to defeat Damien, and it had to happen tonight. It had become a battle for pack leadership, one that would end only in death. He looked back at Bryn, and saw her face had become even more ashen...but there was a fire in her eyes now, that same determined fire that he'd seen so many times before. "He doesn't get to have you," she snapped.

Cash let out his breath, his wolf subsiding at the determination in her voice. Her fear had vanished in the face of her mate being threatened. Just as he needed to protect her, she needed to protect him. She was still vulnerable, but her anger would help keep his wolf under control.

He looked back at Jace. "Come up slowly," he said. "Don't make me kill you."

Jace met his gaze. "Kill me if you need to. That's an order."

Cash nodded. "I understand."

Jace nodded, then reached up to grab the sides of the trap door. His fingers wrapped around the steel, and for a split second, both men stared at each other. Then Cash stood up and held out his hand.

Jace took the offering. Both men grabbed each other's wrists, and Cash hauled him out and into the room. He landed lightly on his feet, with the same grace he always had. The jeans Cash had given him were loose, hanging low on his hips. His chest was chiseled as always, but he'd lost weight from his time in jail. Cash knew it wasn't from the lack of food. It was because no wolf could survive captivity. They needed to be free to run, to hunt, to live according to their own rules. The wasteland of his eyes reflected the torment of a man who had betrayed every moral he possessed, and Cash knew then that Jace might never recover from having killed that woman. Anger roiled through him, and he looked at Drake, who was standing behind Jace.

His friend's face was grim, and he knew that Drake had come to the same conclusion that he had. Jace had broken the night he'd killed that woman, and he might never recover.

Jace was trembling, cold in a heated cabin. He swore and grabbed a sweatshirt for his alpha. Silently, he handed it to him. Jace glanced at him, then took it.

As he did so, Cash walked over to Bryn and pulled her against him. She was shaking violently, and sweat was beading on her forehead. Her hands were trembling, but her gun was still pointed at Jace, her finger hovering on the trigger.

Cash gently put his hand on her wrist. "It's okay, babe."

She said nothing, her jaw taut, her muscles tense, not taking her gaze off Jace for even a split second. Her face was shocked and horrified, as if she were in the presence of a monster. Cash's heart sank at the expression on her face, realizing that was exactly how she saw Jace. He considered Jace his family.

Jace shrugged the sweatshirt over his head and glanced over at them. He saw Bryn's face, and anguish raked across his face. "I'm sorry," he said.

Bryn jumped when he spoke, and the gun shook in her hand. Drake swore, and Jace tensed. The tension level in the room was off the charts, and Cash knew that in seconds, bad shit was going to happen. "Bryn," he said softly. "Give me the gun."

She shook her head, tears sliding down her cheeks. "I can't stop seeing what he did. I saw it. I heard her screams. I smelled her blood. I watched him tear her throat from her body."

Torment flashed over Jace's face. "I know. I relive it every day." He held out his arms to the side like he was strung up on a cross and then went down to his knees. "Pull the trigger, Bryn. Just do it. End both our nightmares."

"Don't," Drake said, inching closer to Jace. "Don't do it. Both of you, stop."

Cash swore under his breath, his hands itching to grab the gun, but afraid she'd accidentally fire it if he startled her. "Bryn, they're my family. Don't do it." Drake was close to Jace now, both men within target range of the silver bullets in her gun. Despite his intense emotional control, fear began to trickle through Cash. The only people he cared about in the entire fucking world were in this room. If she fired on one of them, the wolves would come out. Self-defense was an instinct that couldn't be suppressed. Even if Jace asked her to shoot him, his wolf wouldn't be so ready to die. She would become the enemy instantly.

"I can't stop seeing it," she said. "He—"

"I know what he did," he interrupted, trying to keep his voice gentle enough not to startle her, but strong enough to drag her from her memories, "but can't you see how it affected him? It's broken him. *He didn't do it on purpose*, any more than you killed your mother."

Her gaze snapped to him in anguish. "What? My mother? You bring her into this?"

He knew that was a tough place to go, but he also knew that she had to go there. "You still blame yourself for her death, *but it wasn't your fault*. If you can forgive Jace, you can forgive yourself. Let go."

Tears brimmed in her eyes, but her hands were still shaking. "I didn't mean to kill her."

"I know, babe. I know you didn't." He held out his hand. "If you kill Jace, it will hurt just the same. You're scared of him, and you should be, but you know in his heart, he's a good man. Don't do it to yourself or to him. I'll keep you safe, but you have to do the forgiving. Forgive him, and forgive yourself, for the deaths that neither of you were responsible for."

The sirens on his security system began to wail, and she jumped again, swinging back toward Jace, who hadn't moved.

Drake ran over to the computer and checked the screen. He looked up at Cash. "They're coming. Some in the tunnel, others outside."

Damien had already arrived.

Cash swore, unable to move while Bryn still had the gun aimed at Jace. "We will all die if we don't work together," he said. "Shoot him later, but give us a chance first."

"Shoot me now," Jace said.

"Shut the fuck up, Jace," Drake snapped.

Cash swore, but Jace repeated his request, staring at Bryn when he said it. "Shoot me," he said, pain etched in his voice. "No one is safe with me. I couldn't stop myself before. It could happen again. *End it.*"

Tears were streaming down Bryn's cheeks, silent rivulets of pain, and terror. Cash heard engines outside, and car doors slamming. Son of a bitch. They were out of time.

Chapter Eleven

BRYN COULDN'T TAKE her gaze off Jace's face. There was so much guilt in his eyes, so much pain, so much regret. She felt his anguish deep inside, because it was what she lived with every second of every day. Over and over and over again she relived the car crash, and the sickening thud of her mother's head hitting the dashboard. Over and over again she dreamed of that horrific moment when the car had slid out of control, her own screams, so loud she couldn't hear her mother's, that moment when the car became still, and she looked over at her mom and realized she'd killed her.

The face she saw in the mirror every day looked exactly like Jace's did in that moment, raking across her heart like razor-sharp claws. "It doesn't ever go away," she whispered to him. "It never goes away."

Anguish flashed over his face. "I might do it again," he said, his voice low and tormented. "Don't let me."

Bryn was vaguely aware of Cash talking to her, and she could hear beeping in the distance, but all she could see and hear was Jace's face and his words, and the past that was gripping her so tightly. So much blood. Her mom's. Jace's victim. So much loss that had never stopped eating away at her, and she could see on Jace's face that it was killing him the same way.

He carried so much pain, that she knew, she knew deep in her heart, that he hadn't done it intentionally, any more than she'd killed her mother intentionally. She'd suffered so much. She'd tried to kill herself once when she was eighteen, but she'd been rushed off to the hospital and saved. She'd always been grateful she'd been saved that day, even in her darkest moments, but seeing Jace like that before her made her see that she hadn't come far enough. Cash was right. She still tormented herself, and suddenly, she didn't want to live like that anymore...and she didn't want him to suffer the same. It was too horrible to live like that. Too horrible to die for a mistake that could never be undone. "We can't do this," she said quietly. "God help us, Jace, we can't live like this."

Slowly, her hands still shaking, she let the gun drop.

Disappointment flashed over Jace's face, but she didn't care. When Cash's arms went around her, she turned into him, pressing her face into his shoulder, and sucking in a deep, trembling breath. She felt as though a thousand lifetimes of pain had finally loosened its grip on her, allowing her to breathe for the first time since the night of the car accident.

Jace's suffering had set her free.

"You're okay, babe." Cash wrapped her up tight in his arms, his strength pouring into her. "You're going to make it now."

"I know." She squeezed her eyes shut, trying to

will away the tears that wanted so desperately to fall. She needed to collapse, and mourn, and cry, drained beyond words, but she knew they didn't have time.

Time was up for all of them.

* * *

Cash breathed deeply, his body shuddering with relief as he held Bryn. Jace was down on his hands and knees, his head down, his shoulders shuddering as he fought his own inner demons that only he could battle. But he'd survived the first hurdle: he was still alive.

"Cash. Come look." Drake was at the computer, scanning the screens.

Keeping his arm around Bryn, Cash walked over to the table. Together, the three of them examined the screen. There were three wolves sprinting through the tunnel, but he didn't recognize any of them. The front was a massive black wolf, rippling with muscle, its body utterly relaxed as it moved so gracefully that it almost didn't look like it was touching the ground when it ran. The two flanking the black wolf were smaller gray ones, still large, but dwarfed by the sheer size of the black one. He watched the black one, a bad feeling settling on his shoulders.

He tightened his arm around Bryn, and set the gun back in her hands. "You know them?"

She wrapped her fingers tightly around the handle, her jaw jutting out as she watched the trio advancing.

"I've never seen them." Drake braced his palms on the table, his face tense as he studied the screen. "Jace? You know them?"

It took Jace a few seconds before he took a deep breath and lurched to his feet. His jaw was taut as he walked over, stopping on the far side of Drake and away from Bryn. His entire body was tense, and Cash felt his fear, a fear of not being able to control himself and hurting Bryn, or turning on Cash and Drake. Instinctively, he moved Bryn to his far side, and Jace's dead eyes watched him do it before his gaze flicked to the computer screen.

He studied the monitor, his brow furrowed in a frown. "I can't see them well enough to make out their features. They're not of our pack, though." He leaned forward, his eyes narrowing. "The gait of the black one looks familiar. I know I've seen it before. See how he's positioned himself relative to the other two? He's alpha. Not just their alpha, but alpha to anyone he meets."

Cash's wolf began to pace again, and his skin became hot. He pulled Bryn closer to him, trying to appease his wolf with her. "Alpha?"

"Yeah." Jace gritted his jaw, the muscle in his cheek flexing. "Damien must have aligned himself with him."

"They're planning to take over our pack," Drake said. "That's what this is about."

Jace said nothing, but his face became even more haunted as the depths of his trusted pack mate's betrayal sank in.

"The black wolf must be the one who controlled you," Cash said. "Damien isn't powerful enough. This one is. Look how he moves. He's more than simply a wolf."

The four of them watched as the wolves loped easily along the passageway, heading toward the cabin with almost languid purpose.

"You think he's controlling Damien?" Jace asked. There was no hope in his voice, however. Just resignation.

Cash thought back to his interactions with Damien. The man had been clear and lucid, consistent with his usual character. "I don't think so," Cash said. "I think Damien is working with this other wolf willingly. He wants power, and this is how he's decided to get it."

He looked over at Jace, and saw his anguished expression as he watched the trio closing in. The man he'd chosen to protect his pack was betraying them, which meant Jace had failed his pack. As the alpha, his duty to protect his pack trumped all others. He was the one who was ultimately responsible. He'd failed his pack by putting Damien in charge, and he'd failed to protect an innocent woman from himself. The stricken expression on Jace's face said it all.

"We'll fix this," Cash said. "He's not going to win."

"Fuck yeah," Drake agreed.

Jace said nothing, but Cash had the sense that, despite his anguish, his mind was working on a solution. He might feel like he'd failed his pack, but he still had a chance to save them, and he'd give his life to make it happen.

Cash's phone rang suddenly. He pulled it out and looked at it. Damien's name flashed on his screen. He showed the others, and hit speakerphone. "Yeah."

"Join us," Damien said. "Swear your allegiance to Grigori. We can do so much together."

"Grigori?" Jace repeated the name, and Cash saw understanding flash across his face. He looked at Drake and Cash, and Cash knew that Jace knew the other wolf. Jace took the phone from Cash, his voice hard, edged with steel. "Tell Grigori I'll meet him outside in four minutes. Alone. Just the two of us."

There was silence for a moment, then Damien replied. "He agrees. We'll stand down."

Jace hung up the phone, his face even more tense than it had been. But there was no longer apathy. It was a fierce, deadly focus that was ready for a battle to the death.

The wolves in the tunnel immediately changed direction and began racing back toward the exit, suggesting that the black wolf in the tunnel was Grigori. Cash watched them go, silently calculating the wolf's pacing, and strength, trying to get a feel for his movement. If it came down to a fight, the smallest detail could be the difference between dead and alive. "You know him, don't you?" he asked Jace.

He nodded, watching the screen as intently. "Grigori was the son of my alpha when I was young. His father was a depraved bastard who killed for fun, and Grigori was the same way. I left when I was five, knowing even at that age that something was wrong with that pack. They were in the Norwegian forest at the time. Years later, I heard Grigori and his father were eventually killed by some wolf hunters."

"The Norwegian pack?" Cash and Drake exchanged looks. They'd heard of the Norwegian pack before, bloodthirsty wolves who hunted local people mercilessly, turning the area into a nightmare. Many hunters had been sent into the forest to stop them, and none of them had ever returned. Grigori was death itself, a ruthless predator who broke the laws of nature and hunted simply for pleasure. "And now he's here."

"And now he's here," Jace agreed.

Drake whistled softly, and Bryn's fingers wrapped around Cash's wrist. Grigori was in their territory, ready to prey upon their wolves, upon his woman. Cash growled softly and set his hand on the back of

Bryn's neck. "How do we stop him?"

"He'll never stop. He's blood-crazed." Jace looked at them grimly. "He has to die."

There was something about the way Jace said it that made Cash ask the next question. "Can he be killed?"

"No."

* * *

Icy fear gripped Bryn's spine as she watched the black wolf racing down the tunnel toward the exit. He was pure malevolence, merciless evil, and unbelievable power. She wiped her hand on her jeans, trying to dry the sweat from her palms, even as perspiration trickled down her back, like the steady, insidious approach of death.

Cash touched her back, drawing her attention. His face was grim. "There's a second tunnel," he said, setting a pair of car keys in her hand. "It's still secure. Go through the tunnel. I have a truck at the end of it. Get in and get away from here. Give up on the trial. Just go."

Relief rushed through her at the realization that they weren't going to stay and fight him...until she registered the meaning of his words. "You want me to go alone? Leave you behind?"

He cupped her face as Jace and Drake strategized, making preparations. "This is too dangerous, Bryn. Wolves are going to die tonight. Many wolves. You can't be here. I can't protect you." His words were gentle, but his tone was hard and stubborn. He'd shifted from being her lover to being a warrior, one that had no space for her.

"No!" She gripped his wrists, fear hammering at

her. "I just found you. I'm not losing you again—"

"Grigori doesn't simply kill innocent people." His face was grim. "He does things worse than death, especially to women. He's a depraved, sick bastard. He'll kill you, sweetheart, but not soon enough."

Her throat constricted. "If you can't defeat him, you have to leave!"

He shook his head. "I can't walk away from my pack."

"What about me? You can walk away from me, though?" She shoved at his chest, anger surging through her. "You don't get to sacrifice yourself like that, Cash! You made a promise when you made love to me, a promise that, at the very least, includes not throwing your life away in a battle you can't win just because you want to go out a hero!"

Pain flashed across his face, and he caught her wrists. "Bryn." His voice was soft, stripping her of her anger, leaving behind only a stark terror of losing him.

Tears filled her eyes. "I don't want you to die," she whispered.

"I know, babe." He brushed her hair back from her face. "I'm not giving up, but if I fail, if *we* fail, you have to be far away from here. I have to know that if Grigori wins, he'll never find you. Do you understand? You have to *disappear*."

She searched his face. "You make it sound like he'd hunt me down. Why? I'm not a wolf—" Her heart stuttered, and suddenly she understood what Cash wasn't telling her. "I'm the trophy, aren't I? He *is* going to hunt me down, isn't he?"

He hesitated, and then he nodded. "If Damien knew about this cabin, then we can assume he took the time to research me thoroughly. For all we know, Jace's murder of that woman was specifically timed to occur when you were there to witness it. You might have been targeted all along."

She bit her lip. "Because you're the real threat to him, aren't you? He knew that getting rid of Jace wouldn't give him the pack. He had to destroy you as well, didn't he? You're the real alpha, more than Jace even."

He put his finger over her lips. "Jace is my alpha," he said firmly, and without hesitation. "I don't want that job. But I have his back, and everyone knows that. You're mine, and that means taking you defeats me, so yes." His fingers tightened on her arms, his voice becoming more urgent. "You need to go, Bryn."

She wanted to go. God, how she wanted to go, but her gut was telling her that wasn't the answer. "How do you know the second tunnel hasn't been compromised? If Damien knows you so well, won't he think you'll send me away? Aren't I safest here with you?"

Jace walked up to them. "All three of you go," he said. "I'll delay them long enough. Get out. Start over. Fight them when the odds are in your favor. We won't win today. There's too many." He looked at Cash and Drake. "That's an order, as your alpha. Take Bryn and go."

Bryn tensed at Jace's expression. It was hard, cold, and stern, the face of a leader. She knew, they all knew what he was doing. He was going to sacrifice his life for them, because he wanted to die, because he had to do something to atone for what he'd done. She knew that, because that was how she lived too.

"No." Cash glared at Jace. "We stand with you."

Jace's gaze was unyielding. "I knew you would take over someday, Cash. Now is that time. Go. Drake is your second. Protect the rest of the pack from Damien and Grigori. When the time is right, you'll take them down. Today is not that time. If you stay, we all die, and no one will be left to protect the others." His gaze flicked to Bryn, then back to Cash. "An alpha owes his allegiance to those who count on him for protection, which is your pack and your mate. Go."

Cash bunched his fists. "I won't abandon you."

"But you'll abandon your pack, your best friend, and your mate?" Jace walked over and grabbed Cash's shoulders. "If you stay, you betray *me*. I swore to protect the pack, and *this is the only way.*"

Cash's jaw flexed, and Bryn glanced at Drake, who looked equally stunned. She felt their loyalty toward Jace. Leaving him behind meant leaving him to die. They all knew that, and she knew it went against the very fabric of Cash's soul...but so did abandoning the pack and her. Dammit. Why did it have to be like that? Why did someone have to lose? She was so tired of someone losing—

Jace moved suddenly, so fast she didn't have time to react, snatching the gun out of her hands. Cash lunged for it, but it was too late. Jace had control. He pointed it at Cash's forehead, inches away. "Get the hell out of here," he said in a low voice. "If you won't, I'll shoot you, and it will be up to Drake to do what's right. I won't let my pack fall to these bastards. *I won't.*"

Cash tensed, and she felt his skin get hot. "You're a piece of shit," he snapped.

"It's called being an alpha," Jace said. "When you take the job, it's not your life anymore. Get the hell out. Now."

Cash went utterly still, and the temperature in the

room began to rise quickly. Drake didn't move, and Jace didn't either, but all three men were close to shifting.

"Hey," Bryn didn't dare move. "You guys need each other! If you turn on each other, we're all screwed!"

Cash's phone rang, but no one moved.

"I'll get it." Urgency coursed through her as she raced over to the table and grabbed Cash's phone. She had to stall Grigori somehow, or everything would fall apart. She hit speaker. "Hello."

There was a pause. "Is this Bryn?"

She froze as the male voice crept over her skin, terrifying and creepy, like a predator inching its way into her mind.

Cash leapt across the room and grabbed the phone from her hand. "Grigori."

"Ah...Cash." His voice was smooth and dangerous, like a deadly snake gliding through murky waters. "Excellent to meet you. Damien speaks highly of you. You will join our pack?"

"Fuck you. You don't get any of us."

Jace walked up and aimed the gun at Cash. "Hang up the phone."

Cash looked right at him, and Bryn saw the resolution in his eyes. Jace was ready to shoot him. "Fuck you," Cash said to him. "I won't live a life of regret knowing I gave up."

Pride swelled through Bryn at his loyalty, his unwillingness to walk away from helping Jace. She slipped her hand through his, silently telling him that she was there with him. It had gone beyond atonement for the woman who'd died with only Bryn to see it. It was protection of all the other people yet to die, the people like Jace who would be forced to kill others and be tormented forever because of it. She knew suddenly that this was why she'd survived the car accident, because she was meant to stay by Cash and help him make something right.

Jace moved at lightning speed, snatching Bryn from Cash. He locked her against his chest and pressed the gun to her temple. Bryn froze, her heart hammering at the feel of Jace's body against hers. "If you don't go, she dies."

Cash's eyes turned amber instantly and he went utterly still. "Let her go." His voice was like a razor across her skin, deadly and dangerous.

Drake walked up to Cash, his eyes now a pale, icy blue. He stood beside Cash, just as he'd sworn he would do. "Don't do this, Jace. Don't hurt her. Don't shut us out just because you're fucked up from killing that woman. We can do this."

"I can't walk away from the pack," Jace shouted. "They're counting on me—"

Suddenly, music began to play from the phone, and a woman's voice drifted out into the air, so melodic and beautiful that Bryn's breath caught. All three men froze, and the temperature of the air in the cabin shot up. Jace gasped and let her go, stumbling back as he shoved the gun at her. She caught it as he fell to his knees, holding his ears. Beside her, Cash went down to the ground, and so did Drake, covering their ears.

"It's the song," Jace gasped. "Shoot us, Bryn. *Shoot now.*"

With rising horror, she realized that the song coming from the phone was the same one that had triggered Jace's attack. "No!" She lunged for the phone and threw it across the room. It shattered into fragments, and she spun back toward the three men, who were down on their knees, their muscles bulging beneath their skin as they fought to hold onto their humanity.

"Cash!" She reached for him, skidding on the phone fragments, remembering how she'd helped him regain control. If she couldn't get to him in time—

The three men's eyes shifted, and she froze, her heart thundering as their faces began to shift. In a split second, faster than she could process, the men were gone, and in their place were three enormous, deadly wolves. The animals surrounded her, teeth bared, eyes glowing with the same feral hunger that she'd seen in Jace's before he'd killed Melissa. She recognized Jace's brown fur. The light gray one had Drake's icy blue eyes. And a massive dark gray wolf with amber eyes was in front, its lips raised in a snarl that made her blood turn cold. "Cash?"

But it wasn't Cash. Not anymore. It was the same mindless deadly predator that Jace had become, and she was the only target around. Grigori didn't need to convince them to become a part of his pack. He'd already claimed them. He controlled them. He'd already won...because she'd answered the damned phone and exposed them to the song.

Memories of her mothers' death flashed through her mind, and she stumbled back, horrified by what she'd caused. Once again, she'd made a mistake that was going to destroy those she loved. She would be murdered by the man she loved, and Cash would have to live with the guilt and self-hate that he'd killed her for the rest of his life.

Chapter Twelve

THE THREE WOLVES circled her, crouched low, teeth bared, ready to attack.

Bryn gripped the gun, backing away. "Cash," she shouted, her voice cracking with terror. "It's me. Don't do this!" Jace snapped at her ankle, and she yelped and swung the gun toward him. He snarled at her, and for a split second, her vision blurred as terror tried to overtake her.

"Stop it!" She shouted, backing up as she swung the gun from one to the other. Jace was trying to get behind her and Drake was flanking her other side, also snapping at her ankles. Cash stood in front of her, his golden eyes boring into her.

Dear God. He was a wolf. The man she loved was a *wolf*, and he was about to tear her apart. For the first time, she understood what his life was like, why he'd left. There was nothing of him left in the animal. He was pure predator, oblivious to the identity of his prey. He was driven by a darkness greater than his own humanity, needing to slaughter and kill. Dear God, how many times had this happened to him? To Jace? To Drake?

The wolves moved closer, low growls emanating from their powerful chests, but suddenly, for the first time, she didn't see them as enemies. She felt their torment, understood the prison of hell they lived in, the monster that haunted them at every moment. They were men, honorable men, trapped by the monster that Grigori had called forth.

Drake darted in and lunged for her ankle. She jumped away, toward Jace, who snapped at her calf, making her stumble forward as she tried to get away. She realized they were herding her toward Cash, presenting her to him for the kill.

She met his amber gaze, and saw nothing of the man she loved. There was no humanity in his eyes. He was gone. His lip curled up in a low snarl, and the fur on the ruff on his neck puffed up, making him even larger. His eyes were narrowed, his body rigid and taut, ready to spring.

On either side of her, Jace and Drake waited, ready to finish her off once Cash made the first move—

The steel front door that had been locked and alarmed suddenly swung open, but none of the three wolves even turned their heads as two men walked in, one of them fully dressed in jeans, boots, and a long-sleeved black T-shirt. The other was wearing only jeans, his feet bare, a heavy beard on his jaw, his dark green eyes glittering with power. She knew instantly that he was Grigori. As dangerous as Damien was, Grigori's presence dwarfed him.

"Wait." He snapped a command to the wolves surrounding her, and they went into a crouching position, completely at his mercy.

Dear God. Even without the song playing, he had complete control over them. Was the song simply the trigger he used to get access to their minds? Once they shifted, did they belong to him until he let them go? What kind of power was that?

He walked into the room, followed by Damien. Both were tall and muscular, and Grigori had scars raked across his chest, as if he'd been in dozens of fights that had almost killed him. Grigori smiled at her, a thin, terrifying smile that made her stomach turn. "Do you want me to save you?" he asked conversationally.

"Save me? You?" Cash moved even closer to her, his teeth bared. Drake darted in and bit her calf, his teeth grazing over her skin. She yelped and stumbled back, almost falling when Jace nipped her ankle, sending pain shooting through her skin. Cash just watched, moving inexorably closer, saliva dripping from his jaw.

"If I fuck you, you're mine, not his. You live. Cash doesn't have to kill you." Grigori's gaze bore down on her, and revulsion flooded her.

She knew what he was doing. If he stole her from Cash, he showed everyone that he owned Cash. He already controlled him with the music. His control of the pack would be complete. But if he let Cash kill her, it would still show his power, by forcing a wolf to kill his own mate. Either way, he won. Either way, she lost. Cash lost. Everyone lost. Except him.

"You want Cash to live with the guilt of killing you?" Grigori walked further into the room, followed by Damien. Damien's face was impassive and cold, masking his emotions. Was he under Grigori's control, or was he making his own choices? She could see more wolves and men waiting outside. There were ten that she could see, far outnumbering Cash, Jace, and Drake. Dear God. There was no way out. No way to win.

"You want Cash to wake up every day, knowing he killed the woman he loved? How does that feel, Bryn? You want to punish him with what you've lived through?"

Her gaze snapped to Grigori. "How do you know about that?"

"Because I'm very, very good at what I do. Fuck me now, or you die."

She looked down at Cash, who was poised, waiting for the final command. Her fingers closed around the gun, and Grigori laughed softly. "You won't get a shot off," he said, reading her mind. "They'll bite your hand off before you even raise the gun in my direction."

She knew how fast the wolves could move. She'd seen it.

Grigori walked closer, threading himself between the wolves. He came to a stop in front of her, his merciless eyes boring down on her, standing between her and Cash, who still hadn't moved. His eyes were dark green, laced with flecks of gold, as if he never fully shifted back to human form anymore. His dark hair was long, a thin braid woven into it. A black chain encircled his throat, and a massive signet ring adorned his thumb. But it was his eyes she couldn't take her gaze off of. They were the eyes of a madman, of a killer without mercy. He was unmitigated evil, leaching his taint into the very air she was breathing.

Grigori flicked his finger at Cash, who lifted his lips to reveal gleaming white teeth. His amber eyes were fixed on her throat, and she knew that Cash would kill her the instant Grigori released him.

She knew then that Cash was truly lost, trapped by the monster inside. He would never, *ever* allow Grigori near her if he had any choice. Did his mind know what was going on? Was he screaming inside his prison, trying to get free? "You fear Cash so much that you need to destroy him like this?" She asked the question, not because she cared about the answer, but because she needed time, time to figure out what to do—

"I don't want to destroy him. I want to *use* him." Grigori grabbed her arm and yanked her against him, her body slamming into his hard, muscular one. "You don't dare say no," he said, grabbing the back of her hair and jerking her head back. "You know he can't live with killing you. You'll never risk him like that. He's mine, and so are you."

She stared into his depraved eyes, the eyes of a wolf gone mad, and she knew that he would eventually kill her as well. Through sex. Through depravity. There was no end, no salvation, no respite from his madness. "Cash," she whispered. "Don't let him do this." Cash was right behind him. One move and he could kill Grigori.

But Cash didn't move, trapped by Grigori and his wolf.

Grigori smiled. "Mine." He fisted her hair and his eyes glowed with madness.

Madness.

Madness that wasn't in Cash's eyes, even as a wolf caught in the thrall. Cash was trapped, but he wasn't *insane.* She recalled how Jace had taught Cash to win over the monster. She'd seen Cash subdue his wolf earlier. He could do it. She knew he could. Resolution flooded her. "Fuck you," she said. "I believe in him."

Then, she took the biggest leap of faith she'd ever made, and she began to sing the song that had trapped Cash in the first place, a song so powerful that it would break him free of Grigori's hold. The question was, would it plunge him the rest of the way into the abyss, or give him the split second to reclaim himself?

There was a vicious growl from behind Grigori. His eyebrows went up and he casually stepped to the side. "Foolish girl."

As soon as he moved, Cash lunged, teeth bared, heading straight for her throat.

* * *

He could think of nothing but killing. The need raged white-hot in his brain, consuming him, driving him. *He had to kill her now.* His muscles bunched, and he launched himself at the prey that had been tantalizing him for so long, hunger raging through him. He crashed into her, his front paws slamming her to the ground. His jaws latched around her neck—

He froze, shocked by the taste of her skin, and her scent crashing through his senses. She tasted familiar, like something he knew, something important. She smelled of sweat and fear, and something else. Something that mattered to him. Something that he needed. Confusion hammered at his mind, hunger battling for supremacy over something else. Something more basic. Something more important.

Her fingers dug into his fur, and heat surged through him, a deep, penetrating heat that seared its way through his veins, sending pain shooting through him.

"Cash. I need you." Her voice drifted through his mind, chiseling its way past the haze gripping his mind

so fiercely. *"Come back to me. Now."*

His teeth hovered on her delicate skin, a breath from puncturing the soft flesh. He could smell her blood, and he could hear it rushing through her veins, just below the surface. She was his. Defenseless. Ready to die. She wasn't struggling. She wasn't screaming. She'd accepted her fate—

"Cash. Please. I love you. I believe in you. Cash!"

Her voice was angelic, music more beautiful than he'd ever heard. His soul strained in response, fighting to acknowledge her. He didn't want to kill her. This wasn't right. It wasn't right.

Slowly, painfully, summoning every last shred of willpower, he released his grip on her throat and pulled back. He managed to bring her into focus. She was gazing at him, her fingers still in his fur. Memory flooded back to him, and he recognized her. His mate. His woman. *Bryn.*

Her gaze flicked past him, drawing his attention behind him. Instantly, he sensed movement behind him. He whirled around just as Damien lunged at him. Cash charged for him, slamming into the wolf in mid-air. Teeth snapping, the two heavy bodies crashed to the ground. Damien bit his shoulder, ripping flesh, but Cash tore into him, prying the older wolf off him and hurling him across the room.

Damien hit hard, leapt to his feet, and launched himself at Cash.

Get Grigori! Jace's command filled his mind as the alpha launched himself at Damien. *I've got Damien.*

Cash whirled around in time to see Grigori grab Bryn and sprint for the door. *Bryn!* Cash bolted after her. He sensed Drake racing for the intruder at the same time. They leapt simultaneously, their attacked timed perfectly from years of living together, their teeth tearing into Grigori's shoulders, hitting the alpha just as he reached the grass outside.

He threw Bryn aside as he fell, hurling her into his team of snarling wolves. Cash had a split second to decide, and then he cut off to the left, charging after Bryn as she hit the dirt, Drake right behind him. Cash sprang through the air, landing beside Bryn, sinking his teeth into a wolf just as it lunged for her. He threw it aside, and it fell, shifting back into a man as its neck broke from the fall.

Drake attacked another wolf, protecting Bryn's other side. Bryn grabbed a stick and hit a wolf coming from the other side. The three of them fought together, taking down the wolves one by one, until finally, there were none standing. Grigori was not among the dead, and he was no longer present. All that remained of him were tire tracks in the dirt.

Cash braced himself on his legs, panting, pain spinning through his body as Bryn fell to her knees, the stick falling from her hands.

There were still sounds of fighting coming from the cabin, and Drake spun toward the building. *You stay with her. I'll help Jace.*

Cash didn't argue. Damien didn't matter to him anymore. None of it mattered. He just needed Bryn. He walked over to Bryn and pressed his face against her. She wrapped her arms around him and buried her face in his fur, her body shaking violently. "Cash," she whispered. "I knew you would come back to me."

He needed to hold her. He needed to kiss her. He needed to be himself. The effects of the forced shift were still holding him in wolf form, fighting his efforts to shift back. She clung to him, her fingers tight in his fur.

As she held him, he felt his body begin to relax. His muscles lost their tautness, and he felt his body coming back to him, reclaimed by her touch. He tried again, and this time, he shifted easily back into his human form.

Tears filled her eyes as she watched him shift. She was covered in blood, dirt, and sweat. Her shirt was torn, and she had a bruise forming on her cheek...and she'd never looked so beautiful. "Bryn." He crouched in front of her, framing her face in his hands. "I'm so sorry."

She shook her head, her blue eyes glistening. "You won," she said. "You couldn't kill me. I knew you couldn't. I love you, Cash."

He knew she wasn't talking about teenage love. She was talking about the kind of love that bound two souls together for all eternity. The kind of love that was forever, that was about self-sacrifice, commitment, and the kind of peace that came only from trusting someone enough to give them your heart, your soul, and your body. "I know, babe." He bent his head and kissed her gently, ignoring the pain screaming through his body. "I love you, too, Bryn. Always and forever."

Her face lit up, a huge grin illuminating her tear-streaked cheeks. "It's about time you admitted it."

He laughed, tucking her hair behind her ear. "I was trying to protect you from what I am."

Her smile faded. "I know what you are. I've seen the worst of it, haven't I?"

He shrugged, grimacing at the memory of his teeth around her neck. The memory was terrifying...except for the fact he hadn't done it. He'd been in a killing rage, and he hadn't hurt her, not even one bit. "Pretty much. It doesn't get much worse than tonight."

She nodded. "Will you teach me how to shoot a gun? I realized tonight I need to develop better self-defense skills if I'm going to be hanging out with you."

He groaned at the idea of having to face that again, of having her in danger. "I'm going to retire. You and I are heading to the Caribbean islands and forgetting about the wolf thing—"

Before he could finish, Drake walked out of the cabin, in human form. He was naked, his skin slashed in a dozen places. He made it only a few yards before he sank down onto the grass, his muscular body shaking violently. "Damien's dead," he said, bracing himself on his hands, digging his fingers into the dirt. "Jace is in rough shape. I'm not sure he's going to make it." He dragged his hand over his forehead, wiping away a trickle of blood as he raised his head to look at Cash. "Grigori got away, didn't he? He's still out there. He'll be back."

Cash swore, but before he could say anything, Bryn slipped her hand in his. He looked down at her, and his heart softened when he saw her smile. "Your family is mine, too," she said. "You're all I have left. We're not going to abandon them. Besides, you need me. I'm the only one who can bring you back from the edge. We're not going to the Caribbean. We're staying right here."

He touched her cheek. "You're sure?"

She grinned. "Of course I'm sure. You know you want to stay. Just admit it, and let's get Drake some clothes."

Rightness surged through Cash, and he cupped her face, kissing her again, long and hard. "I love you," he whispered.

She beamed back at him. "I know."

"Hey." Drake was lying down in the grass now. "I'm kind of offended that you'd rather make out than keep me from bleeding out. Just wanted to point that out."

Cash laughed and stood up, staggering slightly to keep his balance. "If we're going to help Jace with the pack, we need to get in better shape." He limped over to Drake and held out his hand. "Come on, buddy. Let's get inside." He hauled Drake to his feet, and the other man staggered, nearly collapsing into him.

Cash caught him just as Bryn walked up, catching Drake's other arm. Together, the three of them limped back to his cabin. The night was a mess, the aftermath would be rough, but Cash felt a sense of deep peace and satisfaction that he hadn't felt since the day he'd turned into a wolf and walked away from the only one he'd ever loved.

He looked over at Bryn as she helped Drake up the steps. "I'm not letting you go again," he said.

She smiled at him. "I'm not letting you go, either, so don't even try."

Rightness pulsed through him. "I'm not going anywhere, babe, unless you're with me."

And he wasn't. He had everything he wanted, everything he needed, and everyone who mattered. It wasn't going to be an easy road ahead, but he wasn't walking away this time. He'd found where he belonged.

As they crossed the threshold into his cabin, he saw Bryn's stuffed reindeer on the floor in the corner. It was Christmas morning now, a Christmas of blood, death, violence, and—

"Merry Christmas, Cash." Bryn smiled at him, a smile so full of warmth and love, that his chest tightened.

—and also love.

That was the other part of Christmas. The best part. The part that would sustain them no matter what came next.

Chapter Thirteen

CASH LOOKED SO handsome in his suit...gorgeous, but still so lethal. No matter how much he cleaned up, Bryn knew she'd always see the wolf in him, the feral dangerous side that had saved her life, the wildly passionate and seductive man who shared her bed every night.

He looked over at her, and smiled, but tension was thick in his green eyes. His jaw was clean-shaven for the first time, and she missed his whiskers. He held her hand tightly in his lap, his fingers entwined with hers.

Beside him sat Drake, also wearing a suit. His arm was in a cast, and he had stitches down the side of his temple and at the base of his neck, from a bite that had nearly killed him. It had been only three days since the fight, but their wounds were already beginning to heal.

They were the only people in the back row of the courtroom. No one sitting near them. No one would even make eye contact, not since Drake and Cash had testified at Jace's trial about how Damien and Grigori had forced them to shift.

They'd both revealed themselves as werewolves to save Jace, a sacrifice that would forever strip them of the anonymity they both burned for. She'd backed them up, her own wounds evidence of the battle they'd fought.

The jury had debated for less than twelve hours, and the verdict was about to be delivered.

Jace was sitting with his head down at the front of the courtroom. He was in even worse shape than Drake from the fight with Damien, his left foot almost completely severed. But even worse was the dead look in his eyes. He was a man without hope, without spirit, without a will to live.

The judge called for attention, and Cash squeezed her hand as the courtroom fell silent, waiting for the verdict. Bryn couldn't take her gaze off Jace, barely listening as the judge began to talk. Jace's head was down. He wasn't even watching the judge. He was just staring at the floor, his shoulders hunched.

She knew he was thinking of Melissa, the woman he'd killed. Cash had told her that he remembered everything he'd done while he'd been in the killing rage, which meant that Jace recalled every moment of killing that woman. Being acquitted would not bring her back, and it would not erase the stains from his soul. She knew that, because she'd lived with the same guilt her whole life. It had taken Cash's love and support to help her past it. There were still times when he woke her up from nightmares and held her until they subsided, and she knew that would continue for a while...but she also knew he would stand by her without question.

Jace didn't have someone to hold him at night. He didn't have someone who would love him with every ounce of her soul. He didn't have someone who would see past the wolf and love him no matter what.

Cash looked over at her, and smiled, a private, tender smile that made her heart tighten. "Thank you for believing in me," he whispered. "Without you, I'm the one who would be sitting up there, with blood on my hands. You were the only thing strong enough to break me free of Grigori."

She traced her finger along his jaw. "I'll always believe in you, Cash."

"I know. I need that." He pressed a kiss to her knuckle. "I can't live without you, Bryn. Life is too dark without you in it."

Warmth flooded her, the kind of warmth that came from deep inside, that couldn't be destroyed by any external force. "Back at ya, big guy."

He chuckled, and kissed her knuckles again. "You're such a sassy little thing."

She grinned. "I know. That's why you love me."

"That, among other reasons," he agreed. "Like your great ass."

She bit her lip to keep from laughing aloud. "Seriously? We're in a courtroom."

"Ssh." Drake elbowed Cash. "The judge is about to deliver the verdict."

They both settled immediately, turning their attention to the front of the courtroom. The judge was solemn and serious in her black robe as she read from the paper the jury had given her. "And for the charge of first degree murder—"

There was a pause, and Bryn held her breath, leaning forward, gripping Cash's hand.

"—we find the defendant, not guilty."

Relief rushed through her, and she felt like jumping to her feet and fist pumping. The crowd gasped, and someone burst into tears in the courtroom. Cash let out a breath, and bowed his head, pressing their joined hands to his lips. Beside him, Drake leaned back in the seat, covering his face with his hands. But Jace flinched, as if someone had hit him.

The judge continued. "For the charge of involuntary manslaughter, we find the defendant not guilty."

The courtroom erupted into a frenzy of discussion, cheers, and shouts of outrage. Cash let out a low whoop, and punched his hands together, sandwiching hers between them. Drake sighed loudly and seemed to sag in his seat, weeks of tension draining from his body. Everyone stood up, talking excitedly, but Jace still didn't move. He just sat there, hunched over, staring at the floor.

Bryn's heart sank at his response. "He doesn't want to be exonerated," she said.

"It's not his fault," Drake snarled. "Grigori is responsible for that woman's murder, not Jace."

"It doesn't matter if it's his fault or not," Cash said, squeezing her hand. "He's taking responsibility for it." He glanced down at Bryn, his face understanding.

Tears clogged her throat, and she knew she would be forever grateful for Cash's acceptance of her past, and his ability to help her let go of her guilt. He was a lethal protector, but he was also a man of deep emotions and compassion, despite the rawness of his childhood.

Jace's lawyer stood up and began shaking hands, but still Jace didn't move. "He's not going to be okay," she said, her throat tight. "Look at him."

Cash squeezed her hand. "He is going to be okay, because he has us."

Drake stood up. "Damn right he does. Let's go get

our boy." He walked out into the aisle, ignoring the whispered looks and the way people moved out of his way. Bryn hurried after him, and Cash stayed right beside her, always keeping his body close enough to her to shield her, a habit she knew he'd never stop, at least not until Grigori was no longer a threat.

The three of them reached Jace, who looked up as they approached, clearly sensing their presence. His eyes were empty, his face sunken and weathered. "It doesn't change anything," he said.

"No, it doesn't." Cash held out his hand. "You were innocent all along, and you still are. Let's go, Jace. It's time to get out of here."

For a long moment, Jace just stared at Cash's hand, then he finally locked wrists with Cash, and let Cash pull him to his feet. Drake handed him his crutches, and emotion flashed across his face. Deep, raw emotion that showed Drake's intense loyalty toward Jace. Like Cash, Drake had a heart that he kept carefully hidden, but she knew it was there.

Three men, so powerful, so deadly, so loyal that they would sacrifice anything for those they loved.

They waited for Jace to extricate himself from behind the table, but just as he reached them, a loud crash sounded from the other side of the room. Instantly, the three men formed a tight circle around her, shielding her on all sides with their bodies.

"Sorry!" One of the security guards called out, and she saw that a table had collapsed. The crowd dispersed, and her three escorts relaxed, moving away from her again, not far, but enough to give her space. Except for Cash, who put his arm around her, keeping her tight against his side as they moved through the crowds of people wanting to interview the three werewolves.

Werewolves who had just shown everyone, including herself, that they were her family, her protectors, her home. Cash pressed a kiss to her hair, and she smiled up at him. He grinned back, a wicked gleam that promised that when they were alone, he was going to show her exactly how important she was to him.

And she knew she was going to love every second of it.

About The Author

Hailed by J.R. Ward as a "paranormal star," *New York Times* and *USA Today* bestselling author Stephanie Rowe is the author of more than forty-five novels, and she's a four-time nominee for the RITA® award, the highest award in romance fiction.

For a complete booklist, visit www.stephanierowe.com.

Keep up with the latest Stephanie Rowe news by signing up for her private news letter at:
http://stephanierowe.com/connect.php.

Facebook
www.facebook.com/StephanieRoweBooks

Twitter @StephanieRowe2

For more information on Stephanie and her books, visit her on the web at www.stephanierowe.com.

Also by Stephanie Rowe

www.ingramcontent.com/pod-product-compliance
Lightning Source LLC
Chambersburg PA
CBHW020351130626
46549CB00006B/2260